Selected Stories by
SAKI

D1670143

Books in this Series:

Selected Stories by
SAKI

RUPA

Published by
Rupa Publications India Pvt. Ltd 2014
7/16, Ansari Road, Daryaganj
New Delhi 110002

Sales Centres:
Allahabad Bengaluru Chennai
Hyderabad Jaipur Kathmandu
Kolkata Mumbai

Selection and Introduction copyright © Terry O'Brien 2014

ISBN: 978-81-291-3138-6

First impression 2014

10 9 8 7 6 5 4 3 2 1

Printed at Shree Maitrey Printech Pvt. Ltd., Noida

CONTENTS

INTRODUCTION

Saki was the pen name of British author Hector Hugh Munro.

'Much in less' is the present-day mantra of writing. It is a great time to remember a writer like Saki who often said more in the two thousand or so words of a short story than many others have in a lifetime. It is for the terse brilliance of his short stories that he is remembered almost a hundred years after his death.

Hector Hugh Munro (Saki) (18 December 1870–13 November 1916) was a master of the short story that is a mixture of humorous satire, irony and the macabre. The stupidities and hypocrisy of conventional society are tersely presented in his stories. His mastery in writing short stories can be compared to that of O. Henry.

- 'The Mouse' portrays what happens when a man is on a train, sharing his compartment with a woman, and finds that there is a mouse climbing up the leg of his pants. And he can't get it out without taking his pants at least partly off!
- In 'Mrs Packletide's Tiger', Mrs Packletide wanted to kill a tiger, not because of her lust to kill, but to outshine her close friend who had recently 'been carried' in an aeroplane.
- 'Down Pens' talks about the conflict of whether or not to write people a 'thank you' note every time they decide to go out and purchase you a gift.
- 'The Storyteller' is about a young bachelor sharing a compartment in a train with an old lady, two small girls and

a small boy and how he ends up telling them a very 'improper story'.

- In 'Minister of Grace', a young Duke takes it upon himself to make changes in the political arena by replacing real cabinet member with 'angels' or clones.

- Does colour have anything to do with Nursery Tea and Le Five O'clock? Read 'A Bread and Butter Miss' to find out.

- In 'The Toys of Peace' Harey, at his sister's request, brings toys that have nothing to do with battles and fighting as gifts to his nephew in an effort to foster interests in things other than war.

- Sacrifice, conflict and a ceaseless struggle have made the world what it is. Is that so? Find out in 'A Sacrifice to Necessity'.

- Sletherby thinks he has a great story to tell about the man he encountered on the train. He laid a trap all right, but was 'A Shot in the Dark' on target?

- In 'The East Wing', a house-party with its typical social mix has a breathless hostess, and is bested by a fire in the middle of the night in the east wing of the house.

- 'Gabriel-Ernest' starts with a warning: 'There is a wild beast in your woods'. There was indeed a wild beast in Van Cheele's woods. What was it?

- 'Esmé' is a hunting story quite unlike the others. The Barness tells Clovis of a hyena she and her friend Constance encountered alone in the countryside.

- In 'Tobermory', one guest announces to the other at a country house party that he has perfected a procedure to teach animals human speech; and he demonstrates this on his host's cat, Tobermory.

- In 'The Bull', Tom, a farmer, receives a visit from his half-brother Laurence, who is an artist and a painter of animals. Laurence tells Tom he sold a painting of a bull for £300 when Tom found it difficult to sell a bull for £100!

- 'The Interlopers' is a story of two men whose families have fought over a forest in the eastern Carpathian mountains for generations.

- Read 'The Schartz-Metterklume Method' to find out if there is a method of making children understand history?
- 'The Match-maker' helps find out if in the end all are happy and smarter.
- 'Hermann the Irascible—A Story of the Great Weep' is about a great plague among the royalty in England. There is a big movement in the country to give women the vote; Hermann does not like the idea but does not feel he is in a position to reject the idea either.
- An infant goes missing. What happens next? Read 'The Quest' to know.
- In 'Filboid Studge, the Story of a Mouse that Helped', read how Mark Spayley helped Duncan Dullamy from the disaster of 'Pipenta'.
- In 'The Open Window', Framton Nuttle, a nervous man, has come to stay in the countryside for his health. His sister has given him letters of introduction to families in the neighbourhood. He goes to visit Mrs Soppleton and meet her fifteen-year-old niece.
- In 'The Unrest-Cure', Clovis Sangrail, a sly young man, overhears the complacent middle-aged Huddle complaining of his own addiction to routine and aversion to change. What happens next?

Start a Saki story and you will finish it. Finish one and you will start another, and having finished them all you will never forget them. They remain an addiction because they are so much more than expected.

1

THE MOUSE

Theodoric Voler had been brought up, from infancy to the confines of middle age, by a fond mother whose chief solicitude had been to keep him screened from what she called the coarser realities of life. When she died she left Theodoric alone in a world that was as real as ever, and a good deal coarser than he considered it had any need to be. To a man of his temperament and upbringing even a simple railway journey was crammed with petty annoyances and minor discords, and as he settled himself down in a second-class compartment one September morning he was conscious of ruffled feelings and general mental discomposure. He had been staying at a country vicarage, the inmates of which had been certainly neither brutal nor bacchanalian, but their supervision of the domestic establishment had been of that lax order which invites disaster. The pony carriage that was to take him to the station had never been properly ordered, and when the moment for his departure drew near, the handyman who should have produced the required article was nowhere to be found. In this emergency Theodoric, to his mute but very intense disgust, found himself obliged to collaborate with the vicar's daughter in the task of harnessing the pony, which necessitated groping about in an ill-lighted outbuilding called a stable, and smelling very like one—except in patches where it smelled of mice. Without being actually afraid of mice, Theodoric classed them among the coarser incidents of life, and considered that Providence, with a little exercise of moral courage, might long ago have recognized that they were not indispensable, and have withdrawn them from circulation. As the train glided out of the station Theodoric's nervous imagination accused himself of exhaling a weak odour of stable yard, and possibly of displaying a mouldy straw or two on his unusually well-brushed garments. Fortunately the only other occupation of the compartment, a lady of about the same age as himself, seemed inclined for slumber rather than scrutiny; the train was not due to stop till the terminus was reached, in about an hour's time, and the carriage was of the old-fashioned sort that held no communication with a corridor, therefore no further travelling companions were likely to intrude on Theodoric's semiprivacy. And yet the train had scarcely attained its normal speed before he became reluctantly but vividly aware that he was not alone with the slumbering lady; he was not even alone in his own clothes. A warm, creeping movement over his flesh betrayed the unwelcome and highly resented presence, unseen but poignant, of a strayed mouse, that had evidently dashed into its present retreat during the episode of the pony harnessing. Furtive stamps and shakes and wildly directed pinches failed to dislodge the intruder, whose motto, indeed, seemed to be Excelsior; and the lawful occupant of the clothes lay back against the cushions and endeavoured rapidly to evolve some means for putting an end to the dual ownership. It was unthinkable that he should continue for the space of a whole hour in the horrible position of a Rowton House for vagrant mice-already his imagination had at least doubled the numbers of the alien invasion. On the other hand, nothing less drastic than partial disrobing would ease him of his tormentor, and to undress in the presence of a lady, even for so laudable a purpose, was an idea that made his ear tips tingle in a blush of abject shame. He had never been able to bring himself even to the mild exposure of openwork socks in the presence of the fair sex. And yet—the lady in this case was to all appearances soundly and securely asleep; the mouse, on the other hand, seemed to be trying to crowd a Wanderjahr into a few strenuous minutes. If there is any truth in the theory of transmigration, this particular mouse must certainly have been, in a former state, a member of the Alpine Club. Sometimes in its eagerness it lost its footing and slipped for half an inch or so; and then, in fright, or more probably temper, it bit. Theodoric was goaded into the most audacious undertaking of his life. Crimsoning to the hue of a beetroot and keeping an agonized watch on his slumbering fellow traveller, he swiftly and noiselessly secured the ends of his railway rug to the racks on either side of the carriage, so that a substantial curtain hung athwart the compartment. In the narrow dressing room that he had thus improvised he proceeded with violent haste to extricate himself partially and the mouse entirely from the surrounding casings of tweed and half-wool. As the unravelled mouse gave a wild leap to the floor, the rug, slipping its fastening at either end, also came down with a heart-curdling flop, and almost simultaneously the awakened sleeper opened her eyes. With a movement almost quicker than the mouse's, Theodoric pounced on the rug and hauled its ample folds chin-high over his dismantled person as he collapsed into the farther corner of the carriage. The blood raced and beat in the veins of his neck and forehead, while he waited dumbly for the communication cord to be pulled. The lady, however, contented herself with a silent stare at her strangely muffled companion. How much had she seen, Theodoric queried to himself; and in any case what on earth must she think of his present posture?

'I think I have caught a chill,' he ventured desperately.

'Really, I'm sorry' she replied. 'I was just going to ask you if you would open this window.'

'I fancy it's malaria,' he added, his teeth chattering slightly, as much from fright as from a desire to support his theory.

'I've got some brandy in my holdall, if you'll kindly reach it down for me' said his companion.

'Not for worlds—I mean, I never take anything for it,' he assured her earnestly.

'I suppose you caught it in the tropics?'

Theodoric, whose acquaintance with the tropics was limited to an annual present of a chest of tea from an uncle in Ceylon, felt that even the malaria was slipping from him. Would it be possible, he wondered to disclose the real state of affairs to her in small installments?

'Are you afraid of mice?' he ventured, growing, if possible, more scarlet in the face.

'Not unless they came in quantities. Why do you ask?'

'I had one crawling inside my clothes just now,' said Theodoric in a voice that hardly seemed his own. 'It was a most awkward situation.'

'It must have been, if you wear your clothes at all tight,' she observed. 'But mice have strange ideas of comfort.'

'I had to get rid of it while you were asleep,' he continued. Then, with a gulp, he added, 'It was getting rid of it that brought me to—to this.'

'Surely leaving off one small mouse wouldn't bring on a chill,' she exclaimed, with a levity that Theodoric accounted abominable.

Evidently she had detected something of his predicament, and was enjoying his confusion. All the blood in his body seemed to have mobilized in one concentrated blush, and an agony of abasement, worse than a myriad mice, crept up and down over his soul. And then, as reflection began to assert itself, sheer terror took the place of humiliation. With every minute that passed the train was rushing nearer to the crowded and bustling terminus, where dozens of prying eyes would be exchanged for the one paralyzing pair that watched him from the farther corner of the carriage. There was one slender, despairing chance, which the next few minutes must decide. His fellow traveller might relapse into a blessed slumber. But as the minutes throbbed by that chance ebbed away. The furtive glance which Theodoric stole at her from time to time disclosed only an unwinking wakefulness.

'I think we must be getting near now,' she presently observed.

Theodoric had already noted with growing terror the recurring stacks of small, ugly dwellings that heralded the journey's end. The words acted as a signal. Like a hunted beast breaking cover and dashing madly toward some other haven of momentary safety he threw aside his rug, and struggled frantically into his dishevelled garments. He was conscious of dull suburban stations racing past the window, of a choking, hammering sensation in his throat and heart, and of an icy silence in that corner toward which he dared not look. Then as he sank back in his seat, clothed and almost delirious, the train slowed down to a final crawl, and the woman spoke.

'Would you be so kind,' she asked, 'as to get me a porter to put me into a cab? It's a shame to trouble you when you're feeling unwell, but being blind makes one so helpless at a railway station.'

2

MRS PACKLETIDE'S TIGER

It was Mrs Packletide's pleasure and intention that she should shoot a tiger. Not that the lust to kill had suddenly descended on her, or that she felt that she would leave India safer and more wholesome than she had found it, with one fraction less of wild beast per million of inhabitants. The compelling motive for her sudden deviation towards the footsteps of Nimrod was the fact that Loona Bimberton had recently been carried eleven miles in an aeroplane by an Algerian aviator, and talked of nothing else; only a personally procured tiger-skin and a heavy harvest of Press photographs could successfully counter that sort of thing. Mrs Packletide had already arranged in her mind the lunch she would give at her house in Curzon Street, ostensibly in Loona Bimberton's honour, with a tiger-skin rug occupying most of the foreground and all of the conversation. She had also already designed in her mind the tiger-claw brooch that she was going to give Loona Bimberton on her next birthday. In a world that is supposed to be chiefly swayed by hunger and by love, Mrs Packletide was an exception; her movements and motives were largely governed by dislike of Loona Bimberton.

Circumstances proved propitious. Mrs Packletide had offered a thousand rupees for the opportunity of shooting a tiger without over-much risk or exertion, and it so happened that a neighbouring village could boast of being the favoured rendezvous of an animal of respectable antecedents, which had been driven by the increasing infirmities of age to abandon game-killing and confine its appetite to the smaller domestic animals. The prospect of earning the thousand rupees had stimulated the sporting and commercial instinct of the villagers; children were posted night and day on the outskirts of the local jungle to head the tiger back in the unlikely event of his attempting to roam away to fresh hunting-grounds, and the cheaper kinds of goats were left about with elaborate carelessness to keep him satisfied with his present quarters. The one great anxiety was lest he should die of old age before the date appointed for the memsahib's shoot. Mothers carrying their babies home through the jungle after the day's work in the fields hushed their singing lest they might curtail the restful sleep of the venerable herd-robber.

The great night duly arrived, moonlit and cloudless. A platform had been constructed in a comfortable and conveniently placed tree, and thereon crouched Mrs Packletide and her paid companion, Miss Mebbin. A goat, gifted with a particularly persistent bleat, such as even a partially deaf tiger might be reasonably expected to hear on a still night, was tethered at the correct distance. With an accurately sighted rifle and a thumb-nail pack of patience cards the sportswoman awaited the coming of the quarry.

'I suppose we are in some danger?' said Miss Mebbin.

She was not actually nervous about the wild beast, but she had a morbid dread of performing an atom more service than she had been paid for.

'Nonsense,' said Mrs Packletide; 'it's a very old tiger. It couldn't spring up here even if it wanted to.'

'If it's an old tiger I think you ought to get it cheaper. A thousand rupees is a lot of money.'

Louisa Mebbin adopted a protective elder sister attitude towards money in general, irrespective of nationality or denomination. Her energetic intervention had saved many a rouble from dissipating itself in tips in some Moscow hotel, and francs and centimes clung to her instinctively under circumstances which would have driven them headlong from less sympathetic hands. Her speculations as to the market depreciation of tiger remnants were cut short by the appearance on the scene of the animal itself. As soon as it caught sight of the tethered goat it lay flat on the earth, seemingly less from a desire to take advantage of all available cover than for the purpose of snatching a short rest before commencing the grand attack.

'I believe it's ill,' said Louisa Mebbin, loudly in Hindustani, for the benefit of the village headman, who was in ambush in a neighbouring tree.

'Hush!' said Mrs Packletide, and at that moment the tiger commenced ambling towards his victim.

'Now, now!' urged Miss Mebbin with some excitement; 'if he doesn't touch the goat we needn't pay for it.' (The bait was an extra.)

The rifle flashed out with a loud report, and the great tawny beast sprang to one side and then rolled over in the stillness of death. In a moment a crowd of excited natives had swarmed on to the scene, and their shouting speedily carried the glad news to the village, where a thumping of tom-toms took up the chorus of triumph. And their triumph and rejoicing found a ready echo in the heart of Mrs Packletide; already that luncheon-party in Curzon Street seemed immeasurably nearer.

It was Louisa Mebbin who drew attention to the fact that the goat was in death-throes from a mortal bullet-wound, while no trace of the rifle's deadly work could be found on the tiger. Evidently the wrong animal had been hit, and the beast of prey had succumbed to heart-failure, caused by the sudden report of the rifle, accelerated by senile decay. Mrs Packletide was pardonably annoyed at the discovery; but, at any rate, she was the possessor of a dead tiger, and the villagers, anxious for their thousand rupees, gladly connived at the fiction that she had shot the beast. And Miss Mebbin was a paid companion. Therefore did Mrs Packletide face the cameras with a light heart, and her pictured fame reached from the pages of the *Texas Weekly Snapshot* to the illustrated Monday supplement of the Novoe Vremya. As for Loona Bimberton, she refused to look at an illustrated paper for weeks, and her letter of thanks for the gift of a tiger-claw brooch was a model of repressed emotions. The luncheon-party she declined; there are limits beyond which repressed emotions become dangerous.

From Curzon Street the tiger-skin rug travelled down to the Manor House, and was duly inspected and admired by the county, and it seemed a fitting and appropriate thing when Mrs Packletide went to the County Costume Ball in the character of Diana. She refused to fall in, however, with Clovis's tempting suggestion of a primeval dance party, at which every one should wear the skins of beasts they had recently slain. 'I should be in rather a Baby Bunting condition,' confessed Clovis, 'with a miserable rabbit-skin or two to wrap up in, but then,' he added, with a rather malicious glance at Diana's proportions, 'my figure is quite as good as that Russian dancing boy's.'

'How amused every one would be if they knew what really happened,' said Louisa Mebbin a few days after the ball.

'What do you mean?' asked Mrs Packletide quickly.

'How you shot the goat and frightened the tiger to death,' said Miss Mebbin, with her disagreeably pleasant laugh.

'No one would believe it,' said Mrs Packletide, her face changing colour as rapidly as though it were going through a book of patterns before post-time.

'Loona Bimberton would,' said Miss Mebbin. Mrs Packletide's face settled on an unbecoming shade of greenish white.

'You surely wouldn't give me away?' she asked.

'I've seen a weekend cottage near Darking that I should

rather like to buy,' said Miss Mebbin with seeming irrelevance. 'Six hundred and eighty, freehold. Quite a bargain, only I don't happen to have the money.'

Louisa Mebbin's pretty weekend cottage, christened by her 'Les Fauves,' and gay in summer-time with its garden borders of tiger-lilies, is the wonder and admiration of her friends.

'It is a marvel how Louisa manages to do it,' is the general verdict.

Mrs Packletide indulges in no more big-game shooting.

'The incidental expenses are so heavy,' she confides to inquiring friends.

3

THE STORYTELLER

It was a hot afternoon, and the railway carriage was correspondingly sultry, and the next stop was at Templecombe, nearly an hour ahead. The occupants of the carriage were a small girl, and a smaller girl, and a small boy. An aunt belonging to the children occupied one corner seat, and the further corner seat on the opposite side was occupied by a bachelor who was a stranger to their party, but the small girls and the small boy emphatically occupied the compartment. Both the aunt and the children were conversational in a limited, persistent way, reminding one of the attentions of a housefly that refuses to be discouraged. Most of the aunt's remarks seemed to begin with 'Don't,' and nearly all of the children's remarks began with 'Why?' The bachelor said nothing out loud. 'Don't, Cyril, don't,' exclaimed the aunt, as the small boy began smacking the cushions of the seat, producing a cloud of dust at each blow.

'Come and look out of the window,' she added.

The child moved reluctantly to the window. 'Why are those sheep being driven out of that field?' he asked.

'I expect they are being driven to another field where there is more grass,' said the aunt weakly.

'But there is lots of grass in that field,' protested the boy; 'there's nothing else but grass there. Aunt, there's lots of grass in that field.'

'Perhaps the grass in the other field is better,' suggested the aunt fatuously.

'Why is it better?' came the swift, inevitable question.

'Oh, look at those cows!' exclaimed the aunt. Nearly every field along the line had contained cows or bullocks, but she spoke as though she were drawing attention to a rarity.

'Why is the grass in the other field better?' persisted Cyril.

The frown on the bachelor's face was deepening to a scowl. He was a hard, unsympathetic man, the aunt decided in her mind. She was utterly unable to come to any satisfactory decision about the grass in the other field.

The smaller girl created a diversion by beginning to recite 'On the Road to Mandalay'. She only knew the first line, but she put her limited knowledge to the fullest possible use. She repeated the line over and over again in a dreamy but resolute and very audible voice; it seemed to the bachelor as though someone had had a bet with her that she could not repeat the line aloud two thousand times without stopping. Whoever it was who had made the wager was likely to lose his bet.

'Come over here and listen to a story,' said the aunt, when the bachelor had looked twice at her and once at the communication cord.

The children moved listlessly towards the aunt's end of the carriage. Evidently her reputation as a story-teller did not rank high in their estimation.

In a low, confidential voice, interrupted at frequent intervals by loud, petulant questionings from her listeners, she began an unenterprising and deplorably uninteresting story about a little girl who was good, and made friends with everyone on account of her goodness, and was finally saved from a mad bull by a number of rescuers who admired her moral character.

'Wouldn't they have saved her if she hadn't been good?' demanded the bigger of the small girls. It was exactly the question that the bachelor had wanted to ask.

'Well, yes,' admitted the aunt lamely, 'but I don't think they would have run quite so fast to her help if they had not liked her so much.'

'It's the stupidest story I've ever heard,' said the bigger of the small girls, with immense conviction.

'I didn't listen after the first bit, it was so stupid,' said Cyril.

The smaller girl made no actual comment on the story, but she had long ago recommenced a murmured repetition of her favourite line.

'You don't seem to be a success as a storyteller,' said the bachelor suddenly from his corner.

The aunt bristled in instant defence at this unexpected attack.

'It's a very difficult thing to tell stories that children can both understand and appreciate,' she said stiffly.

'I don't agree with you,' said the bachelor.

'Perhaps you would like to tell them a story,' was the aunt's retort.

'Tell us a story,' demanded the bigger of the small girls.

'Once upon a time,' began the bachelor, 'there was a little girl called Bertha, who was extraordinarily good.'

The children's momentarily aroused interest began at once to flicker; all stories seemed dreadfully alike, no matter who told them.

'She did all that she was told, she was always truthful, she kept her clothes clean, ate milk puddings as though they were jam tarts, learned her lessons perfectly, and was polite in her manners.'

'Was she pretty?' asked the bigger of the small girls.

'Not as pretty as any of you,' said the bachelor, 'but she was horribly good.'

There was a wave of reaction in favour of the story; the word horrible in connection with goodness was a novelty that commended itself. It seemed to introduce a ring of truth that was absent from the aunt's tales of infant life.

'She was so good,' continued the bachelor, 'that she won several medals for goodness, which she always wore, pinned on to her dress. There was a medal for obedience, another medal for punctuality, and a third for good behaviour. They were large metal medals and they clicked against one another as she walked. No other child in the town where she lived had as many as three medals, so everybody knew that she must be an extra good child.'

'Horribly good,' quoted Cyril.

'Everybody talked about her goodness, and the Prince of the country got to hear about it, and he said that as she was so very good she might be allowed once a week to walk in his park, which was just outside the town. It was a beautiful park, and no children were ever allowed in it, so it was a great honour for Bertha to be allowed to go there.'

'Were there any sheep in the park?' demanded Cyril.

'No,' said the bachelor, 'there were no sheep.'

'Why weren't there any sheep?' came the inevitable question arising out of that answer.

The aunt permitted herself a smile, which might almost have been described as a grin.

'There were no sheep in the park,' said the bachelor, 'because the Prince's mother had once had a dream that her son would either be killed by a sheep or else by a clock falling on him. For that reason the Prince never kept a sheep in his park or a clock in his palace.'

The aunt suppressed a gasp of admiration.

'Was the Prince killed by a sheep or by a clock?' asked Cyril.

'He is still alive, so we can't tell whether the dream will come true,' said the bachelor unconcernedly; 'anyway, there were no sheep in the park, but there were lots of little pigs running all over the place.'

'What colour were they?'

'Black with white faces, white with black spots, black all over, grey with white patches, and some were white all over.'

The storyteller paused to let a full idea of the park's treasures sink into the children's imaginations; then he resumed:

'Bertha was rather sorry to find that there were no flowers in the park. She had promised her aunts, with tears in her eyes, that she would not pick any of the kind Prince's flowers, and she had meant to keep her promise, so of course it made her feel silly to find that there were no flowers to pick.'

'Why weren't there any flowers?'

'Because the pigs had eaten them all,' said the bachelor promptly. 'The gardeners had told the Prince that you couldn't have pigs and flowers together, so he decided to have pigs and no flowers.'

There was a murmur of approval at the excellence of the Prince's decision; so many people would have decided the other way.

'There were lots of other delightful things in the park. There were ponds with gold and blue and green fish in them, and trees with beautiful parrots that said clever things at a moment's notice, and humming birds that hummed all the popular tunes of the day. Bertha walked up and down and enjoyed herself immensely, and thought to herself: 'If I were not so extraordinarily good I should not have been allowed to come into this beautiful park and enjoy all that there is to be seen in it,' and her three medals clinked against one another as she walked and helped to remind her how very good she really was. Just then an enormous wolf came prowling into the park to see if it could catch a fat little pig for its supper.'

'What colour was it?' asked the children, amid an immediate quickening of interest.

'Mud-colour all over, with a black tongue and pale grey eyes that gleamed with unspeakable ferocity. The first thing that it saw in the park was Bertha; her pinafore was so spotlessly white and clean that it could be seen from a great distance. Bertha saw the wolf and saw that it was stealing towards her, and she began to wish that she had never been allowed to come into the park. She ran as hard as she could, and the wolf came after her with huge leaps and bounds. She managed to reach a shrubbery of myrtle bushes and she hid herself in one of the thickest of the bushes. The wolf came sniffing among the branches, its black tongue lolling out of its mouth and its pale grey eyes glaring with rage. Bertha was terribly frightened, and thought to herself: 'If I had not been so extraordinarily good I should have been safe in the town at this moment.' However, the scent of the myrtle was so strong that the wolf could not sniff out where Bertha was hiding, and the bushes were so thick that he might have hunted about in them for a long time without catching sight of her, so he thought he might as well go off and catch a little pig instead. Bertha was trembling very much at having the wolf prowling and sniffing so near her, and as she trembled the medal for obedience clinked against the medals for good conduct and punctuality. The wolf was just moving away when he heard the sound of the medals clinking and stopped to listen; they clinked again in a bush quite near him. He dashed into the bush, his pale grey eyes gleaming with ferocity and triumph, and dragged Bertha out and devoured her to the last morsel. All that was left of her were her shoes, bits of clothing, and the three medals for goodness.'

'Were any of the little pigs killed?'

'No, they all escaped.'

'The story began badly,' said the smaller of the small girls, 'but it had a beautiful ending.'

'It is the most beautiful story that I ever heard,' said the bigger of the small girls, with immense decision.

'It is the only beautiful story I have ever heard,' said Cyril.

A dissentient opinion came from the aunt.

'A most improper story to tell to young children! You have undermined the effect of years of careful teaching.'

'At any rate,' said the bachelor, collecting his belongings preparatory to leaving the carriage, 'I kept them quiet for ten minutes, which was more than you were able to do.'

'Unhappy woman!' he observed to himself as he walked down the platform of Templecombe station; 'for the next six months or so those children will assail her in public with demands for an improper story!'

4

DOWN PENS

'HAVE you written to thank the Froplinsons for what they sent us?' asked Egbert.

'No,' said Janetta, with a note of tired defiance in her voice; 'I've written eleven letters today expressing surprise and gratitude for sundry unmerited gifts, but I haven't written to the Froplinsons.'

'Some one will have to write to them,' said Egbert.

'I don't dispute the necessity, but I don't think the some one should be me,' said Janetta. 'I wouldn't mind writing a letter of angry recrimination or heartless satire to some suitable recipient; in fact, I should rather enjoy it, but I've come to the end of my capacity for expressing servile amiability. Eleven letters today and nine yesterday, all couched in the same strain of ecstatic thankfulness: really, you can't expect me to sit down to another. There is such a thing as writing oneself out.'

'I've written nearly as many,' said Egbert, 'and I've had my usual business correspondence to get through, too. Besides, I don't know what it was that the Froplinsons sent us.'

'A William the Conqueror calendar,' said Janetta, 'with a quotation of one of his great thoughts for every day in the year.'

'Impossible,' said Egbert; 'he didn't have three hundred and sixty-five thoughts in the whole of his life, or, if he did, he kept them to himself. He was a man of action, not of introspection.'

'Well, it was William Wordsworth, then,' said Janetta; 'I know William came into it somewhere.'

'That sounds more probable,' said Egbert; 'well, let's collaborate on this letter of thanks and get it done. I'll dictate, and you can scribble it down. Dear Mrs Froplinson—thank you and your husband so much for the very pretty calendar you sent us. It was very good of you to think of us.'''

'You can't possibly say that,' said Janetta, laying down her pen.

'It's what I always do say, and what every one says to me,' protested Egbert.

'We sent them something on the twenty-second,' said Janetta, 'so they simply HAD to think of us. There was no getting away from it.'

'What did we send them?' asked Egbert gloomily.

'Bridge-markers,' said Janetta, 'in a cardboard case, with some inanity about "digging for fortune with a royal spade" emblazoned on the cover. The moment I saw it in the shop I said to myself "Froplinsons" and to the attendant "How much?" When he said "Ninepence," I gave him their address, jabbed our card in, paid tenpence or elevenpence to cover the postage, and thanked heaven. With less sincerity and infinitely more trouble they eventually thanked me.'

'The Froplinsons don't play bridge,' said Egbert.

'One is not supposed to notice social deformities of that sort,' said Janetta; 'it wouldn't be polite. Besides, what trouble did they take to find out whether we read Wordsworth with gladness? For all they knew or cared we might be frantically embedded in the belief that all poetry begins and ends with John Masefield, and it might infuriate or depress us to have a daily sample of Wordsworthian products flung at us.'

'Well, let's get on with the letter of thanks,' said Egbert.

'Proceed,' said Janetta.

'"How clever of you to guess that Wordsworth is our favourite poet,"' dictated Egbert.

Again Janetta laid down her pen.

'Do you realise what that means?' she asked; 'A Wordsworth booklet next Christmas, and another calendar the Christmas after, with the same problem of having to write suitable letters of thankfulness. No, the best thing to do is to drop all further allusion to the calendar and switch off on to some other topic.'

'But what other topic?'

'Oh, something like this: "What do you think of the New Year Honours List? A friend of ours made such a clever remark when he read it." Then you can stick in any remark that comes into your head; it needn't be clever. The Froplinsons won't know whether it is or isn't.'

'We don't even know on which side they are in politics,' objected Egbert; 'and anyhow you can't suddenly dismiss the subject of the calendar. Surely there must be some intelligent remark that can be made about it.'

'Well, we can't think of one,' said Janetta wearily; 'the fact is, we've both written ourselves out. Heavens! I've just remembered Mrs Stephen Ludberry. I haven't thanked her for what she sent.'

'What did she send?'

'I forget; I think it was a calendar.'

There was a long silence, the forlorn silence of those who are bereft of hope and have almost ceased to care.

Presently Egbert started from his seat with an air of resolution. The light of battle was in his eyes.

'Let me come to the writing-table,' he exclaimed.

'Gladly,' said Janetta. 'Are you going to write to Mrs Ludberry or the Froplinsons?'

'To neither,' said Egbert, drawing a stack of notepaper towards him; 'I'm going to write to the editor of every enlightened and influential newspaper in the Kingdom. I'm going to suggest that there should be a sort of epistolary Truce of God during the festivities of Christmas and New Year. From the twenty-fourth of December to the third or fourth of January it shall be considered an offence against good sense and good feeling to write or expect any letter or communication that does not deal with the necessary events of the moment. Answers to invitations, arrangements about trains, renewal of club subscriptions, and, of course, all the ordinary everyday affairs of business, sickness, engaging new cooks, and so forth, these will be dealt with in the usual manner as something inevitable, a legitimate part of our daily life. But all the devastating accretions of correspondence, incident to the festive season, these should be swept away to give the season a chance of being really festive, a time of untroubled, unpunctuated peace and good will.'

'But you would have to make some acknowledgment of presents received,' objected Janetta; 'otherwise people would never know whether they had arrived safely.'

'Of course, I have thought of that,' said Egbert; 'every present that was sent off would be accompanied by a ticket bearing the date of dispatch and the signature of the sender, and some conventional hieroglyphic to show that it was intended to be a Christmas or New Year gift; there would be a counterfoil with space for the recipient's name and the date of arrival, and all you would have to do would be to sign and date the counterfoil, add a conventional hieroglyphic indicating heartfelt thanks and gratified surprise, put the thing into an envelope and post it.'

'It sounds delightfully simple,' said Janetta wistfully, 'but people would consider it too cut-and-dried, too perfunctory.'

'It is not a bit more perfunctory than the present system,' said Egbert; 'I have only the same conventional language of gratitude at my disposal with which to thank dear old Colonel Chuttle for his perfectly delicious Stilton, which we shall devour to the last morsel, and the Froplinsons for their calendar, which we shall never look at. Colonel Chuttle knows that we are grateful for the Stilton, without having to be told so, and the Froplinsons know that we are bored with their calendar, whatever we may say to the contrary, just as we know that they are bored with the bridge-markers in spite of their written assurance that they thanked us for our charming little gift. What is more, the Colonel knows that even if we had taken a sudden aversion to Stilton or been forbidden it by the doctor, we should still have written a letter of hearty thanks around it. So you see the present system of acknowledgment is just as perfunctory and conventional as the counterfoil business would be, only ten times more tiresome and brain-racking.'

'Your plan would certainly bring the ideal of a Happy Christmas a step nearer realization,' said Janetta.

'There are exceptions, of course,' said Egbert, 'people who really try to infuse a breath of reality into their letters of acknowledgment. Aunt Susan, for instance, who writes: "Thank you very much for the ham; not such a good flavour as the one you sent last year, which itself was not a particularly good one. Hams are not what they used to be." It would be a pity to be deprived of her Christmas comments, but that loss would be swallowed up in the general gain.'

'Meanwhile,' said Janetta, 'what am I to say to the Froplinsons?'

5

MINISTERS OF GRACE

Although he was scarcely yet out of his teens, the Duke of Scaw was already marked out as a personality widely differing from others of his caste and period. Not in externals; therein he conformed correctly to type. His hair was faintly reminiscent of Houbigant, and at the other end of him his shoes exhaled the right soupçon of harness-room; his socks compelled one's attention without losing one's respect; and his attitude in repose had just that suggestion of Whistler's mother, so becoming in the really young. It was within that the trouble lay, if trouble it could be accounted, which marked him apart from his fellows. The Duke was religious. Not in any of the ordinary senses of the word; he took small heed of High Church or Evangelical standpoints, he stood outside of all the movements and missions and cults and crusades of the day, uncaring and uninterested. Yet in a mystical-practical way of his own, which had served him unscathed and unshaken through the fickle years of boyhood, he was intensely and intensively religious. His family were naturally, though unobtrusively, distressed about it. 'I am so afraid it may affect his bridge,' said his mother.

The Duke sat in a pennyworth of chair in St. James's Park, listening to the pessimisms of Belturbet, who reviewed the existing political situation from the gloomiest of standpoints.

'Where I think you political spade-workers are so silly,' said the

Duke, 'is in the misdirection of your efforts. You spend thousands of pounds of money, and Heaven knows, how much dynamic force of brain power and personal energy, in trying to elect or displace this or that man, whereas you could gain your ends so much more simply by making use of the men as you find them. If they don't suit your purpose as they are, transform them into something more satisfactory.'

'Do you refer to hypnotic suggestion?' asked Belturbet, with the air of one who is being trifled with.

'Nothing of the sort. Do you understand what I mean by the verb to koepenick? That is to say, to replace an authority by a spurious imitation that would carry just as much weight for the moment as the displaced original; the advantage, of course, being that the koepenick replica would do what you wanted, whereas the original does what seems best in its own eyes.'

'I suppose every public man has a double, if not two or three,' said Belturbet; 'but it would be a pretty hard task to koepenick a whole bunch of them and keep the originals out of the way.'

'There have been instances in European history of highly successful koepenickery,' said the Duke dreamily.

'Oh, of course, there have been False Dimitris and Perkin Warbecks, who imposed on the world for a time,' assented Belturbet, 'but they personated people who were dead or safely out of the way. That was a comparatively simple matter. It would be far easier to pass oneself of as dead Hannibal than as living Haldane, for instance.'

'I was thinking,' said the Duke, 'of the most famous case of all, the angel who koepenicked King Robert of Sicily with such brilliant results. Just imagine what an advantage it would be to have angels deputizing, to use a horrible but convenient word, for Quinston and Lord Hugo Sizzle, for example; How much smoother the Parliamentary machine would work than at present!'

'Now you're talking nonsense,' said Belturbet; 'angels don't exist nowadays, at least, not in that way, so what is the use of dragging them into a serious discussion? It's merely silly.'

'If you talk to me like that I shall just DO it,' said the Duke.

'Do what?' asked Belturbet. There were times when his young friend's uncanny remarks rather frightened him.

'I shall summon angelic forces to take over some of the more troublesome personalities of our public life, and I shall send the ousted originals into temporary retirement in suitable animal organisms. It's not every one who would have the knowledge or the power necessary to bring such a thing off.'

'Oh, stop that inane rubbish,' said Belturbet angrily; 'it's getting wearisome. Here's Quinston coming,' he added, as there approached along the almost deserted path the well-known figure of a young Cabinet Minister, whose personality evoked a curious mixture of public interest and unpopularity.

'Hurry along, my dear man,' said the young Duke to the Minister, who had given him a condescending nod; 'your time is running short,' he continued in a provocative strain; 'the whole inept crowd of you will shortly be swept away into the world's waste-paper basket.'

'You poor little strawberry-leafed nonentity,' said the Minister, checking himself for a moment in his stride and rolling out his words spasmodically; 'who is going to sweep us away, I should like to know? The voting masses are on our side, and all the ability and administrative talent is on our side too. No power of earth or Heaven is going to move us from our place till we choose to quit it. No power of earth or—'

Belturbet saw, with bulging eyes, a sudden void where a moment earlier had been a Cabinet Minister; a void emphasized rather than relieved by the presence of a puffed-out bewildered-looking sparrow, which hopped about for a moment in a dazed fashion and then fell to a violent cheeping and scolding.

'If we could understand sparrow-language,' said the Duke

serenely, 'I fancy we should hear something infinitely worse than 'strawberry-leafed nonentity.'"

'But good Heavens, Eugene,' said Belturbet hoarsely, 'what has become of? Why, there he is! How on earth did he get there?' And he pointed with a shaking finger towards a semblance of the vanished Minister, which approached once more along the unfrequented path.

The Duke laughed.

'It is Quinston to all outward appearance,' he said composedly, 'but I fancy you will find, on closer investigation, that it is an angel understudy of the real article.'

The Angel-Quinston greeted them with a friendly smile.

'How beastly happy you two look sitting there!' he said wistfully.

'I don't suppose you'd care to change places with poor little us,' replied the Duke chaffingly.

'How about poor little me?' said the Angel modestly. 'I've got to run about behind the wheels of popularity, like a spotted dog behind a carriage, getting all the dust and trying to look as if I was an important part of the machine. I must seem a perfect fool to you onlookers sometimes.'

'I think you are a perfect angel,' said the Duke.

The Angel-that-had-been-Quinston smiled and passed on his way, pursued across the breadth of the Horse Guards Parade by a tiresome little sparrow that cheeped incessantly and furiously at him.

'That's only the beginning,' said the Duke complacently; 'I've made it operative with all of them, irrespective of parties.'

Belturbet made no coherent reply; he was engaged in feeling his pulse. The Duke fixed his attention with some interest on a black swan that was swimming with haughty, stiff-necked aloofness amid the crowd of lesser water-fowl that dotted the ornamental water. For all its pride of bearing, something was evidently ruffling and enraging it; in its way it seemed as angry and amazed as the sparrow had been.

At the same moment a human figure came along the pathway. Belturbet looked up apprehensively.

'Kedzon,' he whispered briefly.

'An Angel-Kedzon, if I am not mistaken,' said the Duke. 'Look, he is talking affably to a human being. That settles it.'

A shabbily dressed lounger had accosted the man who had been Viceroy in the splendid East, and who still reflected in his mien some of the cold dignity of the Himalayan snow-peaks.

'Could you tell me, sir, if them white birds is storks or halbatrosses? I had an argyment—'

The cold dignity thawed at once into genial friendliness.

'Those are pelicans, my dear sir. Are you interested in birds? If you would join me in a bun and a glass of milk at the stall yonder, I could tell you some interesting things about Indian birds. Right oh! Now the hill-mynah, for instance—'

The two men disappeared in the direction of the bun stall, chatting volubly as they went, and shadowed from the other side of the railed enclosure by a black swan, whose temper seemed to have reached the limit of inarticulate rage.

Belturbet gazed in an open-mouthed wonder after the retreating couple, then transferred his attention to the infuriated swan, and finally turned with a look of scared comprehension at his young friend lolling unconcernedly in his chair. There was no longer any room to doubt what was happening. The 'silly–talk' had been translated into terrifying action.

'I think a prairie oyster on the top of a stiffish brandy-and-soda might save my reason,' said Belturbet weakly, as he limped towards his club.

It was late in the day before he could steady his nerves sufficiently to glance at the evening papers. The Parliamentary report proved significant reading, and confirmed the fears that he had been trying to shake off. Mr Ap Dave, the Chancellor, whose lively controversial style endeared him to his supporters and embittered him, politically speaking, to his opponents, had risen in his place to make an unprovoked apology for having alluded in a recent speech to certain protesting taxpayers as 'skulkers.' He had realized on reflection that they were in all probability perfectly honest in their inability to understand certain legal technicalities of the new finance laws. The House had scarcely recovered from this sensation when Lord Hugo Sizzle caused a further flutter of astonishment by going out of his way to indulge in an outspoken appreciation of the fairness, loyalty, and straight–forwardness not only of the Chancellor, but of all the members of the Cabinet. A wit had gravely suggested moving the adjournment of the House in view of the unexpected circumstances that had arisen.

Belturbet anxiously skimmed over a further item of news printed immediately below the Parliamentary report: 'Wild cat found in an exhausted condition in Palace yard.'

'Now I wonder which of them—' he mused, and then an appalling idea came to him. 'Supposing he's put them both into the same beast!' He hurriedly ordered another prairie oyster.

Belturbet was known in his club as a strictly moderate drinker; his consumption of alcoholic stimulants that day gave rise to considerable comment.

The events of the next few days were piquantly bewildering to the world at large; to Belturbet, who knew dimly what was happening, the situation was fraught with recurring alarms. The old saying that in politics; it's the unexpected that always happens received a justification that it had hitherto somewhat lacked, and the epidemic of startling personal changes of front was not wholly confined to the realm of actual politics. The eminent chocolate magnate, Sadbury, whose antipathy to the Turf and everything connected with it was a matter of general knowledge, had evidently been replaced by an Angel-Sadbury, who proceeded to electrify the public by blossoming forth as an owner of race-horses, giving as a reason his matured conviction that the sport was, after all, one which gave healthy open-air recreation to large numbers of people drawn from all classes of the community, and incidentally stimulated the important industry of horse-breeding. His colours, chocolate and cream hoops spangled with pink stars, promised to become as popular as any on the Turf. At the same time, in order to give effect to his condemnation of the evils resulting from the spread of the gambling habit among wage-earning classes, who lived for the most part from hand to mouth, he suppressed all betting news and tipsters' forecasts in the popular evening paper that was under his control. His action received instant recognition and support from the Angel-proprietor of the 'EVENING VIEWS,' the principal rival evening halfpenny paper, who forthwith issued an ukase decreeing a similar ban on betting news, and in a short while the regular evening Press was purged of all mention of starting prices and probable winners. A considerable drop in the circulation of all these papers was the immediate result, accompanied, of course, by a falling-off in advertisement value, while a crop of special betting broadsheets sprang up to supply the newly-created want. Under their influence the betting habit became if anything rather more widely diffused than before. The Duke had possibly overlooked the futility of koepenicking the leaders of the nation with excellently intentioned angel under-studies, while leaving the mass of the people in its original condition.

Further sensation and dislocation was caused in the Press world by the sudden and dramatic RAPPROCHEMENT which took place between the Angel-Editor of the SCRUTATOR and the Angel-Editor of the ANGLIAN REVIEW, who not only ceased to criticize and disparage the tone and tendencies of each other's publication, but agreed to exchange editorships for alternating periods. Here again public support was not on the side of the angels; constant readers of the SCRUTATOR complained bitterly of the strong meat which was thrust upon them at fitful intervals in place of the almost vegetarian diet to which they had become confidently accustomed; even those who were not mentally averse to strong meat as a separate course were pardonably annoyed at being supplied with it in the pages of the SCRUTATOR. To be suddenly confronted with a pungent herring salad when one had attuned oneself to tea and toast, or to discover a richly truffled segment of Pate De Foie dissembled in a bowl of bread and milk, would be an experience that might upset the equanimity of the most placidly disposed mortal. An equally vehement outcry arose from the regular subscribers of the ANGLIAN REVIEW who protested against being served from time to time with literary fare which no young person of sixteen could possibly want to devour in secret. To take infinite precautions, they complained, against the juvenile perusal of such eminently innocuous literature was like reading the Riot Act on an uninhabited island. Both reviews suffered a serious falling-off in circulation and influence. Peace hath its devastations as well as war.

The wives of noted public men formed another element of discomfiture which the young Duke had almost entirely left out of his calculations. It is sufficiently embarrassing to keep abreast of the possible wobblings and veerings-round of a human husband, who, from the strength or weakness of his personal character, may leap over or slip through the barriers which divide the parties; for this reason a merciful politician usually marries late in life, when he has definitely made up his mind on which side he wishes his wife to be socially valuable. But these trials were as nothing compared to the bewilderment caused by the Angel-husbands who seemed in some cases to have revolutionized their outlook on life in the interval between breakfast and dinner, without premonition or preparation of any kind, and apparently without realizing the least need for subsequent explanation. The temporary peace which brooded over the Parliamentary situation was by no means reproduced in the home circles of the leading statesmen and politicians. It had been frequently and extensively remarked of Mrs Exe that she would try the patience of an angel; now the tables were reversed, and she unwittingly had an opportunity for discovering that the capacity for exasperating behaviour was not all on one side.

And then, with the introduction of the Navy Estimates, Parliamentary peace suddenly dissolved. It was the old quarrel between Ministers and the Opposition as to the adequacy or the reverse of the Government's naval programme. The Angel-Quinston and the Angel-Hugo Sizzle contrived to keep the debates free from personalities and pinpricks, but an enormous sensation was created when the elegant lackadaisical Halfan Halfour threatened to bring up fifty, thousand stalwarts to wreck the House if the Estimates were not forthwith revised on a Two-Power basis. It was a memorable scene when he rose in his place, in response to the scandalized shouts of his opponents, and thundered forth, 'Gentlemen, I glory in the name of Apache.'

Belturbet, who had made several fruitless attempts to ring up his young friend since the fateful morning in St. James's Park, ran him to earth one afternoon at his club, smooth and spruce and unruffled as ever.

'Tell me, what on earth have you turned Cocksley Coxon into?' Belturbet asked anxiously, mentioning the name of one of the pillars of unorthodoxy in the Anglican Church. 'I don't fancy he BELIEVES in angels, and if he finds an angel preaching orthodox sermons from his pulpit while he's been turned into a fox-terrier, he'll develop rabies in less than no time.'

'I rather think it was a fox-terrier,' said the Duke lazily.

Belturbet groaned heavily, and sank into a chair.

'Look here, Eugene,' he whispered hoarsely, having first looked well round to see that no one was within hearing range, 'you've got to stop it. Consols are jumping up and down like bronchos, and that speech of Halfour's in the House last night has simply startled everybody out of their wits. And then on the top of it, Thistlebery–'

'What has he been saying?' asked the Duke quickly.

'Nothing. That's just what's so disturbing. Every one thought it was simply inevitable that he should come out with a great epoch-making speech at this juncture, and I've just seen on the tape that he has refused to address any meetings at present, giving as a reason his opinion that something more than mere speech-making was wanted.'

The young Duke said nothing, but his eyes shone with quiet exultation.

'It's so unlike Thistlebery,' continued Belturbet; 'at least,' he said suspiciously, 'it's unlike the REAL Thistlebery–'

'The real Thistlebery is flying about somewhere as a vocally-industrious lapwing,' said the Duke calmly; 'I expect great things of the Angel-Thistlebery,' he added.

At this moment there was a magnetic stampede of members towards the lobby, where the tape-machines were ticking out some news of more than ordinary import.

'COUP D'ETAT in the North. Thistlebery seizes Edinburgh Castle. Threatens civil war unless Government expands naval programme.'

In the babel which ensued Belturbet lost sight of his young friend. For the best part of the afternoon he searched one likely haunt after another, spurred on by the sensational posters which the evening papers were displaying broadcast over the West End. 'General Baden-Baden mobilizes Boy-Scouts. Another COUP D'ETAT feared. Is Windsor Castle safe?' This was one of the earlier posters, and was followed by one of even more sinister purport: 'Will the Test-match have to be postponed?' It was this disquietening question which brought home the real seriousness of the situation to the London public, and made people wonder whether one might not pay too high a price for the advantages of party government. Belturbet, questing round in the hope of finding the originator of the trouble, with a vague idea of being able to induce him to restore matters to their normal human footing, came across an elderly club acquaintance who dabbled extensively in some of the more sensitive market securities. He was pale with indignation, and his pallor deepened as a breathless newsboy dashed past with a poster inscribed: 'Premier's constituency harried by moss-troopers. Halfour sends encouraging telegram to rioters. Letchworth Garden City threatens reprisals. Foreigners taking refuge in Embassies and National Liberal Club.'

'This is devils' work!' he said angrily.

Belturbet knew otherwise.

At the bottom of St. James's Street a newspaper motor-cart, which had just come rapidly along Pall Mall, was surrounded by a knot of eagerly talking people, and for the first time that afternoon Belturbet heard expressions of relief and congratulation.

It displayed a placard with the welcome announcement: 'Crisis ended. Government gives way. Important expansion of naval programme.'

There seemed to be no immediate necessity for pursuing the quest of the errant Duke, and Belturbet turned to make his way homeward through St. James's Park. His mind, attuned to the alarums and excursions of the afternoon, became dimly aware that some excitement of a detached nature was going on around him. In spite of the political ferment which reigned in the streets, quite a large crowd had gathered to watch the unfolding of a tragedy that had taken place on the shore of the ornamental water. A large black swan, which had recently shown signs of a savage and dangerous disposition, had suddenly attacked a young gentleman who was walking by the water's edge, dragged him down under the surface, and drowned him before anyone could come to his assistance. At the moment when Belturbet arrived on the spot several park-keepers were engaged in lifting the corpse into a punt. Belturbet stooped to pick up a hat that lay near the scene of the struggle. It was a smart soft felt hat, faintly reminiscent of Houbigant.

More than a month elapsed before Belturbet had sufficiently recovered from his attack of nervous prostration to take an interest once more in what was going on in the world of politics. The Parliamentary Session was still in full swing, and a General Election was looming in the near future. He called for a batch of morning papers and skimmed rapidly through the speeches of the Chancellor, Quinston, and other Ministerial leaders, as well as those of the principal Opposition champions, and then sank back in his chair with a sigh of relief. Evidently the spell had ceased to act after the tragedy which had overtaken its invoker. There was no trace of angel anywhere.

6

A BREAD AND BUTTER MISS

'Starling Chatter and Oakhill have both dropped back in the betting,' said Bertie van Tahn, throwing the morning paper across the breakfast table.

'That leaves Nursery Tea practically favourite,' said Odo Finsberry.

'Nursery Tea and Pipeclay are at the top of the betting at present,' said Bertie, 'but that French horse, Le Five O'Clock, seems to be fancied as much as anything. Then there is Whitebait, and the Polish horse with a name like some one trying to stifle a sneeze in church; they both seem to have a lot of support.'

'It's the most open Derby there's been for years,' said Odo.

'It's simply no good trying to pick the winner on form,' said Bertie; 'one must just trust to luck and inspiration.'

'The question is whether to trust to one's own inspiration, or somebody else's. Sporting Swank gives Count Palatine to win, and Le Five O'Clock for a place.'

'Count Palatine—that adds another to our list of perplexities. Good morning, Sir Lulworth; have you a fancy for the Derby by any chance?'

'I don't usually take much interest in turf matters,' said Sir Lulworth, who had just made his appearance, 'but I always like to have a bet on the Guineas and the Derby. This year, I confess, it's rather difficult to pick out anything that seems markedly better than anything else. What do you think of Snow Bunting?'

'Snow Bunting?' said Odo, with a groan, 'there's another of them. Surely, Snow Bunting has no earthly chance?'

'My housekeeper's nephew, who is a shoeing-smith in the mounted section of the Church Lads' Brigade, and an authority on horseflesh, expects him to be among the first three.'

'The nephews of housekeepers are invariably optimists,' said Bertie; 'it's a kind of natural reaction against the professional pessimism of their aunts.'

'We don't seem to get much further in our search for the probable winner,' said Mrs de Claux; 'the more I listen to you experts the more hopelessly befogged I get.'

'It's all very well to blame us,' said Bertie to his hostess; 'you haven't produced anything in the way of an inspiration.'

'My inspiration consisted in asking you down for Derby week,' retorted Mrs de Claux; 'I thought you and Odo between you might throw some light on the question of the moment.'

Further recriminations were cut short by the arrival of Lola Pevensey, who floated into the room with an air of gracious apology.

'So sorry to be so late,' she observed, making a rapid tour of inspection of the breakfast dishes.

'Did you have a good night?' asked her hostess with perfunctory solicitude.

'Quite, thank you,' said Lola; 'I dreamt a most remarkable dream.'

A flutter, indicative of general boredom; went round the table. Other people's dreams are about as universally interesting as accounts of other people's gardens, or chickens, or children.

'I dreamt about the winner of the Derby,' said Lola.

A swift reaction of attentive interest set in.

'Do tell us what you dreamt,' came in a chorus.

'The really remarkable thing about it is that I've dreamt it two nights running,' said Lola, finally deciding between the allurements of sausages and kedgeree; 'that is why I thought it worth mentioning. You know, when I dream things two or three nights in succession, it always means something; I have special powers in that way. For instance, I once dreamed three times that a winged lion was flying through the sky and one of his wings dropped off, and he came to the ground with a crash; just afterwards the Campanile at Venice fell down. The winged lion is the symbol of Venice, you know,' she added for the enlightenment of those who might not be versed in Italian heraldry. 'Then,' she continued, 'just before the murder of the King and Queen of Servia I had a vivid dream of two crowned figures walking into a slaughter-house by the banks of a big river, which I took to be the Danube; and only the other day–'

'Do tell us what you've dreamt about the Derby,' interrupted Odo impatiently.

'Well, I saw the finish of the race as clearly as anything; and one horse won easily, almost in a canter, and everybody cried out "Bread and Butter wins! Good old Bread and Butter." I heard the name distinctly, and I've had the same dream two nights running.'

'Bread and Butter,' said Mrs de Claux, 'now, whatever horse can that point to? Why–of course: Nursery Tea!'

She looked round with the triumphant smile of a successful unraveller of mystery.

'How about Le Five O'Clock?' interposed Sir Lulworth.

'It would fit either of them equally well,' said Odo; 'can you remember any details about the jockey's colours? That might help us.'

'I seem to remember a glimpse of lemon sleeves or cap, but I can't be sure,' said Lola, after due reflection.

'There isn't a lemon jacket or cap in the race,' said Bertie, referring to a list of starters and jockeys; 'can't you remember anything about the appearance of the horse? If it were a thick-set animal, this bread and butter would typify Nursery Tea; and if it were thin, of course, it would mean Le Five O'Clock.'

'That seems sound enough,' said Mrs de Claux; 'do think, Lola dear, whether the horse in your dream was thin or stoutly built.'

'I can't remember that it was one or the other,' said Lola; 'one wouldn't notice such a detail in the excitement of a finish.'

'But this was a symbolic animal,' said Sir Lulworth; 'if it were to typify thick or thin bread and butter surely it ought to have been either as bulky and tubby as a shire cart-horse; or as thin as a heraldic leopard.'

'I'm afraid you are rather a careless dreamer,' said Bertie resentfully.

'Of course, at the moment of dreaming I thought I was witnessing a real race, not the portent of one,' said Lola; 'otherwise I should have particularly noticed all helpful details.'

'The Derby isn't run till tomorrow,' said Mrs de Claux; 'do you think you are likely to have the same dream again tonight? If so; you can fix your attention on the important detail of the animal's appearance.'

'I'm afraid I shan't sleep at all tonight,' said Lola pathetically; 'every fifth night I suffer from insomnia, and it's due tonight.'

'It's most provoking,' said Bertie; 'of course, we can back both horses, but it would be much more satisfactory to have all our money on the winner. Can't you take a sleeping-draught, or something?'

'Oakleaves, soaked in warm water and put under the bed, are recommended by some,' said Mrs de Claux.

'A glass of Benedictine, with a drop of eau-de-Cologne–' said Sir Lulworth.

'I have tried every known remedy,' said Lola, with dignity; 'I've been a martyr to insomnia for years.'

'But now we are being martyrs to it,' said Odo sulkily; 'I

particularly want to land a big coup over this race.'

'I don't have insomnia for my own amusement,' snapped Lola.

'Let us hope for the best,' said Mrs de Claux soothingly; 'to-night may prove an exception to the fifth-night rule.'

But when breakfast time came round again Lola reported a blank night as far as visions were concerned.

'I don't suppose I had as much as ten minutes' sleep, and, certainly, no dreams.'

'I'm so sorry, for your sake in the first place, and ours as well,' said her hostess; 'do you think you could induce a short nap after breakfast? It would be so good for you—and you MIGHT dream something. There would still be time for us to get our bets on.'

'I'll try if you like,' said Lola; 'it sounds rather like a small child being sent to bed in disgrace.'

'I'll come and read the Encyclopaedia Britannica to you if you think it will make you sleep any sooner,' said Bertie obligingly.

Rain was falling too steadily to permit of outdoor amusement, and the party suffered considerably during the next two hours from the absolute quiet that was enforced all over the house in order to give Lola every chance of achieving slumber. Even the click of billiard balls was considered a possible factor of disturbance, and the canaries were carried down to the gardener's lodge, while the cuckoo clock in the hall was muffled under several layers of rugs. A notice, 'Please do not Knock or Ring,' was posted on the front door at Bertie's suggestion, and guests and servants spoke in tragic whispers as though the dread presence of death or sickness had invaded the house. The precautions proved of no avail: Lola added a sleepless morning to a wakeful night, and the bets of the party had to be impartially divided between Nursery Tea and the French Colt.

'So provoking to have to split our bets,' said Mrs de Claux, as her guests gathered in the hall later in the day, waiting for the result of the race.

'I did my best for you,' said Lola, feeling that she was not getting her due share of gratitude; 'I told you what I had seen in my dreams, a brown horse, called Bread and Butter, winning easily from all the rest.'

'What?' screamed Bertie, jumping up from his sea, 'a brown horse! Miserable woman, you never said a word about it being a brown horse.'

'Didn't I?' faltered Lola; 'I thought I told you it was a brown horse. It was certainly brown in both dreams. But I don't see what the colour has got to do with it. Nursery Tea and Le Five O'Clock are both chestnuts.'

'Merciful Heaven! Doesn't brown bread and butter with a sprinkling of lemon in the colours suggest anything to you?' raged Bertie.

A slow, cumulative groan broke from the assembly as the meaning of his words gradually dawned on his hearers.

For the second time that day Lola retired to the seclusion of her room; she could not face the universal looks of reproach directed at her when Whitebait was announced winner at the comfortable price of fourteen to one.

7

THE TOYS OF PEACE

'Harvey,' said Eleanor Bope, handing her brother a cutting from a London morning paper of the 19th of March, 'just read this about children's toys, please; it exactly carries out some of our ideas about influence and upbringing.'

'In the view of the National Peace Council,' ran the extract, 'there are grave objections to presenting our boys with regiments of fighting men, batteries of guns, and squadrons of 'Dreadnoughts'. Boys, the Council admits, naturally love fighting and all the panoply of war...but that is no reason for encouraging, and perhaps giving permanent form to, their primitive instincts. At the Children's Welfare Exhibition, which opens at Olympia in three weeks' time, the Peace Council will make an alternative suggestion to parents in the shape of an exhibition of 'peace toys.' In front of a specially-painted representation of the Peace Palace at The Hague will be grouped, not miniature soldiers but miniature civilians, not guns but ploughs and the tools of industry... It is hoped that manufacturers may take a hint from the exhibit, which will bear fruit in the toy shops.'

'The idea is certainly an interesting and very well-meaning one,' said Harvey; 'whether it would succeed well in practice–'

'We must try,' interrupted his sister; 'you are coming down to us at Easter, and you always bring the boys some toys, so that will be an excellent opportunity for you to inaugurate the new experiment. Go about in the shops and buy any little toys and models that have special bearing on civilian life in its more peaceful aspects. Of course you must explain the toys to the children and interest them in the new idea. I regret to say that the 'Siege of Adrianople' toy, that their Aunt Susan sent them, didn't need any explanation; they knew all the uniforms and flags, and even the names of the respective commanders, and when I heard them one day using what seemed to be the most objectionable language they said it was Bulgarian words of command; of course it MAY have been, but at any rate I took the toy away from them. Now I shall expect your Easter gifts to give quite a new impulse and direction to the children's minds; Eric is not eleven yet, and Bertie is only nine-and-a-half, so they are really at a most impressionable age.'

'There is primitive instinct to be taken into consideration, you know,' said Henry doubtfully, 'and hereditary tendencies as well. One of their great-uncles fought in the most intolerant fashion at Inkerman—he was specially mentioned in dispatches, I believe–and their great-grandfather smashed all his Whig neighbours' hot houses when the great Reform Bill was passed. Still, as you say, they are at an impressionable age. I will do my best.'

On Easter Saturday Harvey Bope unpacked a large, promising-looking red cardboard box under the expectant eyes of his nephews. 'Your uncle has brought you the newest thing in toys,' Eleanor had said impressively, and youthful anticipation had been anxiously divided between Albanian soldiery and a Somali camel-corps. Eric was hotly in favour of the latter contingency. 'There would be Arabs on horseback,' he whispered; 'the Albanians have got jolly uniforms, and they fight all day long, and all night, too, when there's a moon, but the country's rocky, so they've got no cavalry.'

A quantity of crinkly paper shavings was the first thing that met the view when the lid was removed; the most exiting toys always began like that. Harvey pushed back the top layer and drew forth a square, rather featureless building.

'It's a fort!' exclaimed Bertie.

'It isn't, it's the palace of the Mpret of Albania.' said Eric, immensely proud of his knowledge of the exotic title; 'It's got no windows, you see, so that passers-by can't fire in at the Royal Family.'

'It's a municipal dustbin,' said Harvey hurriedly; 'you see all the refuse and litter of a town is collected there, instead of lying about and injuring the health of the citizens.'

In an awful silence he disinterred a little lead figure of a man in black clothes.

'That,' he said, 'is a distinguished civilian, John Stuart Mill. He was an authority on political economy.'

'Why?' asked Bertie.

'Well, he wanted to be; he thought it was a useful thing to be.'

Bertie gave an expressive grunt, which conveyed his opinion that there was no accounting for tastes.

Another square building came out, this time with windows and chimneys.

'A model of the Manchester branch of the Young Women's Christian Association,' said Harvey.

'Are there any lions?' asked Eric hopefully. He had been reading Roman history and thought that where you found Christians you might reasonably expect to find a few lions.

'There are no lions,' said Harvey. 'Here is another civilian, Robert Raikes, the founder of Sunday schools, and here is a model of a municipal wash-house. These little round things are loaves backed in a sanitary bakehouse. That lead figure is a sanitary inspector, this one is a district councillor, and this one is an official of the Local Government Board.'

'What does he do?' asked Eric wearily.

'He sees to things connected with his Department,' said Harvey. 'This box with a slit in it is a ballot-box. Votes are put into it at election times.'

'What is put into it at other times?' asked Bertie.

'Nothing. And here are some tools of industry, a wheelbarrow and a hoe, and I think these are meant for hop-poles. This is a model beehive, and that is a ventilator, for ventilating sewers. This seems to be another municipal dust-bin–no, it is a model of a school of art and public library. This little lead figure is Mrs Hemans, a poetess, and this is Rowland Hill, who introduced the system of penny postage. This is Sir John Herschel, the eminent astrologer.'

'Are we to play with these civilian figures?' asked Eric.

'Of course,' said Harvey, 'these are toys; they are meant to be played with.'

'But how?'

It was rather a poser. 'You might make two of them contest a seat in Parliament,' said Harvey, 'and have an election–'

'With rotten eggs, and free fights, and ever so many broken heads!' exclaimed Eric.

'And noses all bleeding and everybody drunk as can be,' echoed Bertie, who had carefully studied one of Hogarth's pictures.

'Nothing of the kind,' said Harvey, 'nothing in the least like that. Votes will be put in the ballot-box, and the Mayor will count them– and he will say which has received the most votes, and then the two candidates will thank him for presiding, and each will say that the contest has been conducted throughout in the pleasantest and most straightforward fashion, and they part with expressions of mutual esteem. There's a jolly game for you boys to play. I never had such toys when I was young.'

'I don't think we'll play with them just now,' said Eric, with an entire absence of the enthusiasm that his uncle had shown; 'I think perhaps we ought to do a little of our holiday task. It's history this time; we've got to learn up something about the Bourbon period in France.'

'The Bourbon period,' said Harvey, with some disapproval in his voice.

'We've got to know something about Louis the Fourteenth,' continued Eric; 'I've learnt the names of all the principal battles already.'

This would never do. 'There were, of course, some battles fought during his reign,' said Harvey, 'but I fancy the accounts of them were much exaggerated; news was very unreliable in those days, and there were practically no war correspondents, so generals and commanders could magnify every little skirmish they engaged in till they reached the proportions of decisive battles. Louis was really famous, now, as a landscape gardener; the way he laid out Versailles was so much admired that it was copied all over Europe.'

'Do you know anything about Madame Du Barry?' asked Eric; 'Didn't she have her head chopped off?'

'She was another great lover of gardening,' said Harvey, evasively; 'in fact, I believe the well known Rose Du Barry was named after her, and now I think you had better play for a little and leave your lessons till later.'

Harvey retreated to the library and spent some thirty or forty minutes in wondering whether it would be possible to compile a history, for use in elementary schools, in which there should be no prominent mention of battles, massacres, murderous intrigues, and violent deaths. The York and Lancaster period and the Napoleonic era would, he admitted to himself, present considerable difficulties, and the Thirty Years' War would entail something of a gap if you left it out altogether. Still, it would be something gained if, at a highly impressionable age, children could be got to fix their attention on the invention of calico printing instead of the Spanish Armada or the Battle of Waterloo.

It was time, he thought, to go back to the boys' room, and see how they were getting on with their peace toys. As he stood outside the door he could hear Eric's voice raised in command; Bertie chimed in now and again with a helpful suggestion.

'That is Louis The Fourteenth,' Eric was saying, 'that one in knee-breeches, that Uncle said invented Sunday schools. It isn't a bit like him, but it'll have to do.'

'We'll give him a purple coat from my paintbox by and by,' said Bertie.

'Yes, an' red heels. That is Madame de Maintenon, that one he called Mrs Hemans. She begs Louis not to go on this expedition, but he turns a deaf ear. He takes Marshal Saxe with him, and we must pretend that they have thousands of men with them. The watchword is Qui vive? and the answer is L'etat c'est moi—that was one of his favourite remarks, you know. They land at Manchester in the dead of the night, and a Jacobite conspirator gives them the keys of the fortress.'

Peeping in through the doorway Harvey observed that the municipal dustbin had been pierced with holes to accommodate the muzzles of imaginary cannon, and now represented the principal fortified position in Manchester; John Stuart Mill had been dipped in red ink, and apparently stood for Marshal Saxe.

'Louis orders his troops to surround the Young Women's Christian Association and seize the lot of them. "Once back at the Louvre and the girls are mine," he exclaims. We must use Mrs Hemans again for one of the girls; she says "Never," and stabs Marshal Saxe to the heart.'

'He bleeds dreadfully,' exclaimed Bertie, splashing red ink liberally over the facade of the Association building.

'The soldiers rush in and avenge his death with the utmost savagery. A hundred girls are killed'—here Bertie emptied the remainder of the red ink over the devoted building–'and the surviving five hundred are dragged off to the French ships. "I have lost a Marshal," says Louis, "but I do not go back empty-handed."'

Harvey stole away from the room, and sought out his sister.

'Eleanor,' he said, 'the experiment—'

'Yes?'

'Has failed. We have begun too late.'

8

A SACRIFICE TO NECESSITY

Alicia Pevenly sat on a garden seat in the rose-walk at Chopehanger, enjoying the valedictory mildness of a warm October morning, and experiencing the atmosphere of mental complacency that descends on a woman who has breakfasted well, is picturesquely dressed, and has reached forty-two in pleasant insidious stages. The loss of her husband some ten years ago had woven a thread of tender regret into her life pattern, but for the most part she looked on the world and its ways with placid acquiescent amiability. The income on which she and her seventeen-year-old daughter lived and kept up appearances was small, almost inconveniently small, perhaps, but with due management and a little forethought it sufficed. Contriving and planning gained a certain amount of zest from the fact that there was only such a slender margin of shillings to be manipulated.

'There is all the difference in the world,' Mrs Pevenly would say to herself, 'between being badly off and merely having to be careful.'

Regarding her own personal affairs with a measured tranquillity, she did not let the larger events of the world disturb her peace of mind. She took a warm, but quite impersonal interest, in the marriage of Prince Arthur of Connaught, thereby establishing her claim to be considered a woman with broad sympathies and intelligently in touch with the age in which she lived. On the other hand, she was not greatly stirred by the question whether Ireland should or should not be given Home Rule, and she was absolutely indifferent as to where the southern frontier of Albania should be drawn or whether it should be drawn at all; if there had ever been a combative strain in her nature it had never been developed.

Mrs Pevenly had finished her breakfast at about half-past nine, by which time her daughter had not put in an appearance; as the hostess and most of the members of the house-party were equally late, Beryl's slackness could not be regarded as a social sin, but her mother thought it was a pity to lose so much of the fine October morning. Beryl Pevenly had been described by someone as the 'Flapper incarnate', and the label summed her up accurately. Her mother already recognised that she was disposed to be a law unto herself; what she did not yet realise was that Beryl was extremely likely to be a law-giver to any weaker character with whom she might come into contact.

'She is only a child yet,' Mrs Pevenly would say to herself, forgetting that seventeen and seventy are about the two most despotic ages of human life.

'Ah, finished breakfast at last!' she called out in mock re–proof as her daughter came out to join her in the rose-walk; 'If you had gone to bed in good time these last two evenings, as I did, you would not be so tired in the mornings. It has been so fresh and charming out here, while all you silly people have been lying in bed. I hope you weren't playing bridge for high stakes, my dear!'

There was a tired defiant look in Beryl's eyes that drew forth the anxious remark.

'Bridge? No, we started with a rubber or two the night before last,' said Beryl, 'but we switched off to baccarat. Rather a mistake for some of us.'

'Beryl, you haven't been losing?' asked Mrs Pevenly with increased anxiety in her voice.

'I lost quite a lot the first evening,' said Beryl, 'and as I couldn't possibly pay back my losses I simply punted the next evening to try and get them back; I've come to the conclusion that baccarat is not my game. I came a bigger cropper on the second evening than on the first.'

'Beryl, this is awful! I've very angry with you. Tell me quickly, how much have you lost?'

Beryl looked at a slip of paper that she was twisting and untwisting in her hands.

'Three hundred and ten the first night, seven hundred and sixteen the second,' she announced.

'Three hundred what?'

'Pounds.'

'Pounds?', screamed the mother; 'Beryl, I don't believe you. Why, that is a thousand pounds!'

'A thousand and twenty-six, to be exact,' said Beryl.

Mrs Pevenly was too frightened to cry.

'Where do you suppose,' she asked, 'that we could raise a thousand pounds, or anything like a thousand pounds? We are living at the top of our income, we are practising all sorts of economies, we simply couldn't subtract a thousand pounds from our little capital. It would ruin us.'

'We should be socially ruined if it got about that we played for stakes that we couldn't or wouldn't pay; no one would ask us anywhere.'

'How came you to do such a dreadful thing?' wailed the mother.

'Oh, it's no use asking those sort of questions,' said Beryl; 'the thing is done. I suppose I inherit a gambling instinct from some of you.'

'You certainly don't,' exclaimed Mrs Pevenly hotly; 'your father never touched cards or cared anything about horse-racing, and I don't know one game of cards from another.'

'These things skip a generation sometimes, and come out all the stronger in the next batch,' said Beryl; 'how about that uncle of yours who used to get up a sweepstake every Sunday at school as to which of the Books of the Bible the text of the sermon would be taken from? If he wasn't a keen gambler I've never heard of one.'

'Don't let's argue,' faltered the elder woman, 'let's think of what is to be done. How many people do you owe the money to?'

'Luckily it's all due to one person, Ashcombe Gwent' said Beryl; 'he was doing nearly all the winning on both nights. He's rather a good sort in his way, but unluckily he isn't a bit well off, and one couldn't expect him to overlook the fact that money was owing to him. I fancy he's just as much of an adventurer as we are.'

'We are not adventurers,' protested Mrs Pevenly.

'People who come to stay at country houses and play for stakes that they've no prospect of paying if they lose, are adventurers,' said Beryl, who seemed determined to include her mother in any moral censure that might be applied to her own conduct.

'Have you said anything to him about the difficulty you are in?'

'I have. That's what I've come to tell you about. We had a talk this morning in the billiard-room after breakfast. It seems there is just one way out of the tangle. He's inclined to be amorous.'

'Amorous!' exclaimed the mother.

'Matrimonially amorous,' said the daughter; 'in fact, without either of us having guessed it, it appears that he's the victim of an infatuation.'

'He has certainly been polite and attentive,' said Mrs Pevenly; 'he is not a man who says much, but he listens to what one has to say. And do you mean he really wants to marry–?'

'That is exactly what he does want,' said Beryl. 'I don't know that he is the sort of husband that one would rave about, but I gather that he has enough to live on—as much as we're accustomed to, anyhow, and he's quite presentable to look at. The alternative is selling out a big chunk of our little capital; I should have to go and be a governess or typewriter or something, and you would have to do needlework. From just making things do, and paying rounds of visits and having a fairly good time, we should sink suddenly to the position of distressed gentlefolk. I don't know what you think, but I'm inclined to consider that the marriage proposition is the least objectionable.'

Mrs Pevenly took out her handkerchief.

'How old is he?' she asked.

'Oh, thirty-seven or thirty-eight; a year or two older perhaps.'

'Do you like him?'

Beryl laughed.

'He's not in the least my style,' she said.

Mrs Pevenly began to weep.

'What a deplorable situation' she sobbed; 'what a sacrifice for the sake of a miserable sum of money and social considerations! To think that such a tragedy should happen in our family. I've often read about such things in books, a girl being forced to marry a man she didn't care about because of some financial disaster–'

'You shouldn't read such trashy books,' pronounced Beryl.

'But now it's really happening!' exclaimed the mother; 'my own child's life to be sacrificed by marriage to a man years older than herself, whom she doesn't care the least bit about, and because—'

'Look here,' interrupted Beryl. 'I don't seem to have made this clear. It isn't me that he wants to marry. 'Flappers' don't appeal to him, he told me. Mature womanhood is his particular line, and it's you that he's infatuated about.'

'Me!'

For the second time that morning Mrs Pevenly's voice rose to a scream.

'Yes, he said you were his ideal, a ripe, sun-warmed peach, delicious and desirable, and a lot of other metaphors that he probably borrowed from Swinburne or Edmund Jones. I told him that under other circumstances I shouldn't have held out much hope of his getting a favourable response from you, but that as we owed him a thousand and twenty-six pounds you would probably consider a matrimonial alliance the most convenient way of discharging the obligation. He's coming out to speak to you himself in a few minutes, but I thought I'd better come and prepare you first.'

'But, my dear—'

'Of course, you hardly know the man, but I don't think that matters. You see, you've been married before and a second husband is always something of an anti-climax. Here is Ashcombe. I think I'd better leave you two together. You must have a lot you want to say to each other.'

The wedding took place quietly some eight weeks later. The presents were costly, if not numerous, and consisted chiefly of a cancelled I.O.U., the gift of the bridegroom to the bride's daughter.

9

A SHOT IN THE DARK

Philip Sletherby settled himself down in an almost empty railway carriage, with the pleasant consciousness of being embarked on an agreeable and profitable pilgrimage. He was bound for Brill Manor, the country residence of his newly achieved acquaintance, Mrs Saltpen-Jago. Honoria Saltpen-Jago was a person of some social importance in London, of considerable importance and influence in the county of Chalkshire. The county of Chalkshire, or, at any rate, the eastern division of it, was of immediate personal interest to Philip Sletherby; it was held for the Government in the present Parliament by a gentleman who did not intend to seek re-election, and Sletherby was under serious consideration by the party managers as his possible successor. The majority was not a large one, and the seat could not be considered safe for a Ministerial candidate, but there was an efficient local organisation, and with luck the seat might be held. The Saltpen-Jago influence was not an item which could be left out of consideration, and the political aspirant had been delighted at meeting Honoria at a small and friendly luncheon-party, still more gratified when she had asked him down to her country house for the following Friday-to-Tuesday. He was obviously 'on approval', and if he could secure the goodwill of his hostess he might count on the nomination as an assured thing. If he failed to find favour in her eyes—well, the local leaders would probably cool off in their embryo enthusiasm for him.

Among the passengers dotted about on the platform, awaiting their respective trains, Sletherby espied a club acquaintance, and beckoned him up to the carriage-window for a chat.

'Oh, you're staying with Mrs Saltpen-Jago for the week-end, are you? I expect you'll have a good time; she has the reputation of being an excellent hostess. She'll be useful to you, too, if that Parliamentary project — hullo, you're off. Good-bye.'

Sletherby waved good-bye to his friend, pulled up the window, and turned his attention to the magazine lying on his lap. He had scarcely glanced at a couple of pages, however, when a smothered curse caused him to glance hastily at the only other occupant of the carriage. His travelling companion was a young man of about two-and-twenty, with dark hair, fresh complexion, and the blend of smartness and disarray that marks the costume of a 'nut' who is bound on a rustic holiday. He was engaged in searching furiously and ineffectually for some elusive or non-existent object; from time to time he dug a sixpenny bit out of a waistcoat pocket and stared at it ruefully, then recommenced the futile searching operations. A cigarette-case, matchbox, latchkey, silver pencil case, and railway ticket were turned out on to the seat beside him, but none of these articles seemed to afford him satisfaction; he cursed again, rather louder than before.

The vigorous pantomime did not draw forth any remark from Sletherby, who resumed his scrutiny of the magazine.

'I say!' exclaimed a young voice presently, 'Didn't I hear you say you were going down to stay with Mrs Saltpen-Jago at Brill Manor? What a coincidence! My mater, you know. I'm coming on there on Monday evening, so we shall meet. I'm quite a stranger; haven't seen the mater for six months at least. I was away yachting last time she was in Town. I'm Bertie, the second son, you know. I say, it's an awfully lucky coincidence that I should run across someone who knows the mater just at this particular moment. I've done an damned awkward thing.'

'You've lost something, haven't you?' said Sletherby

'Not exactly, but left behind, which is almost as bad; just as inconvenient, anyway. I've come away without my sovereign-purse, with four quid in it, all my worldly wealth for the moment. It was in my pocket all right, just before I was starting, and then I wanted to seal a letter, and the sovereign purse happens to have my crest on it, so I whipped it out to stamp the seal with, and, like a double-distilled idiot, I must have left it on the table. I had some silver loose in my pocket, but after I'd paid for a taxi and my ticket I'd only got this forlorn little sixpence left. I'm stopping at a little country inn near Brondquay for three days' fishing; not a soul knows me there, and my weekend bill, and tips, and cab to and from the station, and my ticket on to Brill, that will mount up to two or three quid, won't it? If you wouldn't mind lending me two pound ten, or three for preference, I shall be awfully obliged. It will pull me out of no end of a hole.'

'I think I can manage that,' said Sletherby, after a moment's hesitation.

'Thanks awfully. It's jolly good of you. What a lucky thing for me that I should have chanced across one of the mater's friends. It will be a lesson to me not to leave my exchequer lying about anywhere, when it ought to be in my pocket. I suppose the moral of the whole thing is don't try and convert things to purposes for which they weren't intended. Still, when a sovereign-purse has your crest on it—'

'What is your crest, by the way?' Sletherby asked, carelessly.

'Not a very common one,' said the youth; 'a demi-lion holding a cross-crosslet in its paw.'

'When your mother wrote to me, giving me a list of trains, she had, if I remember rightly, a greyhound courant on her notepaper,' observed Sletherby. There was a tinge of coldness in his voice.

'That is the Jago crest,' responded the youth promptly; 'the demi-lion is the Saltpen crest. We have the right to use both, but I always use the demi-lion, because, after all, we are really Salt—pens.'

There was silence for a moment or two, and the young man began to collect his fishing tackle and other belongings from the rack.

'My station is the next one,' he announced.

'I've never met your mother,' said Sletherby suddenly, 'though we've corresponded several times. My introduction to her was through political friends. Does she resemble you at all in feature? I should rather like to be able to pick her out if she happened to be on the platform to meet me.'

'She's supposed to be like me. She has the same dark brown hair and high colour; it runs in her family. I say, this is where I get out.'

'Good-bye,' said Sletherby.

'You've forgotten the three quid,' said the young man, opening the carriage-door and pitching his suit-case on to the platform.

'I've no intention of lending you three pounds, or three shillings,' said Sletherby severely.

'But you said—'

'I know, I did. My suspicions hadn't been roused then, though I hadn't necessarily swallowed your story. The discrepancy about the crests put me on my guard, notwithstanding the really brilliant way in which you accounted for it. Then I laid a trap for you; I told you that I had never met Mrs Saltpen-Jago. As a matter of fact I met her at lunch on Monday last. She is a pronounced blonde.'

The train moved on, leaving the soi-disant cadet of the Saltpen-Jago family cursing furiously on the platform.

'Well, he hasn't opened his fishing expedition by catching a flat,' chuckled Sletherby. He would have an entertaining story to recount at dinner that evening, and his clever little trap would earn him applause as a man of resource and astuteness. He was still telling his adventure in imagination to an attentive audience of dinner guests when the train drew up at his destination. On the platform he was greeted sedately by a tall footman, and noisily by Claude People, K.C., who had apparently travelled down by the same train.

'Hullo, Sletherby! You spending the weekend at Brill? Good. Excellent. We'll have a round of golf together to-morrow; I'll give you your revenge for Hoylake. Not a bad course here, as inland courses go. Ah, here we are; here's the car waiting for us, and very nice, too!'

The car which won the K.C.'s approval was a sumptuous-looking vehicle, which seemed to embody the last word in elegance, comfort, and locomotive power. Its graceful lines and symmetrical design masked the fact that it was an enormous wheeled structure, combining the features of a hotel lounge and an engine-room.

'Different sort of vehicle to the post-chaise in which our grandfathers used to travel, eh?' exclaimed the lawyer appreciatively. And for Sletherby's benefit he began running over the chief points of perfection in the fitting and mechanism of the car.

Sletherby heard not a single word, noted not one of the details that were being expounded to him. His eyes were fixed on the door panel, on which were displayed two crests: a greyhound courant and a demi-lion holding in its paw a cross-crosslet.

The K.C. was not the sort of man to notice an absorbed silence on the part of a companion. He had been silent himself for nearly an hour in the train, and his tongue was making up for lost time. Political gossip, personal anecdote, and general observation flowed from him in an uninterrupted stream as the car sped along the country roads; from the inner history of the Dublin labour troubles and the private life of the Prince Designate of Albania he progressed with an easy volubility to an account of an alleged happening at the ninth hole at Sandwich, and a verbatim report of a remark made by the Duchess of Pathshire at a Tango tea. Just as the car turned in at the Brill entrance gates the K.C. captured Sletherby's attention by switching his remarks to the personality of their hostess.

'Brilliant woman, level-headed, a clear thinker, knows exactly when to take up an individual or a cause, exactly when to let him or it drop. Influential woman, but spoils herself and her chances by being too restless. No repose. Good appearance, too, till she made that idiotic change.'

'Change?' queried Sletherby, 'what change?'

'What change? You don't mean to say– Oh, of course, you've only known her just lately. She used to have beautiful dark brown hair, which went very well with her fresh complexion; then one day, about five weeks ago, she electrified everybody by appearing as a brilliant blonde. Quite ruined her looks. Here we are. I say, what's the matter with you? You look rather ill.'

10

THE EAST WING

IT was early February and the hour was somewhere about two in the morning. Most of the house-party had retired to bed. Lucien Wattleskeat had merely retired to his bedroom where he sat over the still vigorous old-age of a fire, balancing the entries in his bridge-book. They worked out at seventy-eight shillings on the right side, as the result of two evenings' play, which was not so bad, considering that the stakes had been regrettably low.

Lucien was a young man who regarded himself with an undemonstrative esteem, which the undiscerning were apt to mistake for indifference. Several women of his acquaintance were on the look-out for nice girls for him to marry, a vigil in which he took no share.

The atmosphere of the room was subtly tinged with an essence of tuberose, and more strongly impregnated with the odour of wood-fire smoke. Lucien noticed this latter circumstance as he finished his bridge-audit, and also noticed that the fire in the grate was not a wood one, neither was it smoking.

A stronger smell of smoke blew into the room a moment later as the door opened, and Major Boventry, pyjama-clad and solemnly excited, stood in the doorway.

'The house is on fire!' he exclaimed.

'Oh!' said Lucien, 'Is that it? I thought perhaps you had come to talk to me. If you would shut the door the smoke wouldn't pour in so.'

'We ought to do something,' said the Major with conviction.

'I hardly know the family,' said Lucien, 'but I suppose one will be expected to be present, even though the fire does not appear to be in this wing of the house.'

'It may spread to here,' said the Major.

'Well, let's go and look at it,' assented Lucien, 'though it's against my principles to meet trouble half-way.'

'Grasp your nettle, that's what I say,' observed Boventry.

'In this case, Major, it's not our nettle,' retorted Lucien, carefully shutting the bedroom door behind him.

In the passage they encountered Canon Clore, arrayed in a dressing-gown of Albanian embroidery, which might have escaped remark in a Te Deum service in the Cathedral of the Assumption at Moscow, but which looked out of place in the corridor of an English country house. But then, as Lucien observed to himself, at a fire one can wear anything.

'The house is on fire,' said the Canon, with the air of one who lends dignity to a fact by according it gracious recognition.

'It's in the east wing, I think,' said the Major.

'I suppose it is another case of suffragette militancy,' said the Canon. 'I am in favour of women having the vote myself, even if, as some theologians assert, they have no souls. That, indeed, would furnish an additional argument for including them in the electorate, so that all sections of the community, the soulless and the souled, might be represented, and, being in favour of the female vote, I am naturally in favour of militant means to achieve it. Belonging as I do to a Church Militant, I should be inconsistent if I professed to stand aghast at militant methods in vote-winning warfare. But, at the same time, I cannot resist pointing out that the women who are using violent means to wring the vote-right from a reluctant legislature are destroying the value of the very thing for which they are struggling. A vote is of no conceivable consequence to anybody unless it carries with it the implicit understanding that majority-rule is the settled order of the day, and the militants are actively engaged in demonstrating that any minority armed with a box of matches and a total disregard of consequences can force its opinions and its wishes on an indifferent or hostile community. It is not merely manor-houses that they are destroying, but the whole fabric of government by ballot-box.'

'Oughtn't we to be doing something about the fire?' said Major Boventry.

'I was going to suggest something of the sort myself,' said the Canon stiffly.

'Tomorrow may be too late, as the advertisements in the newspapers say,' observed Lucien.

In the hall they met their hostess, Mrs Gramplain.

'I'm so glad you have come,' she said; 'servants are so little help in an emergency of this kind. My husband has gone off in the car to summon the fire-brigade.'

'Haven't you telephoned to them?' asked the Major.

'The telephone unfortunately is in the east wing,' said the hostess; 'so is the telephone-book. Both are being devoured by the flames at this moment. It makes one feel dreadfully isolated. Now if the fire had only broken out in the west wing instead, we could have used the telephone and had the fire-engines here by now.'

'On the other hand,' objected Lucien, 'Canon Clore and Major Boventry and myself would probably have met with the fate that has overtaken the telephone-book. I think I prefer the present arrangement.'

'The butler and most of the other servants are in the dining-room, trying to save the Raeburns and the alleged Van Dyke,' continued Mrs Gramplain, 'and in that little room on the first landing, cut off from us by the cruel flames, is my poor darling Eva? Eva of the golden hair. Will none of you save her?'

'Who is Eva of the golden hair?' asked Lucien.

'My daughter,' said Mrs Gramplain.

'I didn't know you had a daughter,' said Lucien, 'and really I don't think I can risk my life to save some one I've never met or even heard about. You see, my life is not only wonderful and beautiful to myself, but if my life goes, nothing else really matters to me. I don't suppose you can realise that, to me, the whole world as it exists today, the Ulster problem, the Albanian tangle, the Kikuyu controversy, the wide field of social reform and Antarctic exploration, the realms of finance, and research and international armaments, all this varied and crowded and complex world, all comes to a complete and absolute end the moment my life is finished. Eva might be snatched from the flames and live to be the grandmother of brilliant and charming men and women; but, as far as I should be concerned, she and they would no more exist than a vanished puff of cigarette smoke or a dissolved soda-water bubble. And if, in losing my life, I am to lose her life and theirs, as far as I personally am concerned with them, why on earth should I, personally, risk my life to save hers and theirs?'

'Major Boventry,' exclaimed Mrs Gramplain, 'you are not clever, but you are a man with honest human feelings. I have only known you for a few hours, but I am sure you are the man I take you for. You will not let my Eva perish.'

'Lady,' said the Major stumblingly, 'I would gladly give my life to rescue your Eva, or anybody's Eva for the matter of that, but my life is not mine to give. I am engaged to the sweetest little woman in the world. I am everything to her. What would my poor little Mildred say if they brought her news that I had cast away my life in an endeavour, perhaps fruitless, to save some unknown girl in a burning country house?'

'You are like all the rest of them,' said Mrs Gramplain bitterly; 'I thought that you, at least, were not stupid. It shows how rash it is to judge a man by his bridge-play. It has been like this all my life,' she continued in dull, level tones; 'I was married, when little more than a child, to my husband, and there has never been any real bond of affection between us. We have been polite and considerate to one another, nothing more. I sometimes think that if we had had a child things might have been different.'

'But...your daughter Eva?' queried the Canon, and the two other men echoed his question.

'I have never had a daughter,' said the woman quietly, yet, amid the roar and crackle of the flames, her voice carried, so that not a syllable was lost. 'Eva is the outcome of my imagination. I so much wanted a little girl, and at last I came to believe that she really existed. She grew up, year by year, in my mind, and when she was eighteen I painted her portrait, a beautiful young girl with masses of golden hair. Since that moment the portrait has been Eva. I have altered it a little with the changing years. She is twenty-one now, and I have repainted her dress with every incoming fashion. On her last birthday I painted her a pair of beautiful diamond earrings. Every day I have sat with her for an hour or so, telling her my thoughts, or reading to her. And now she is there, alone with the flames and the smoke, unable to stir, waiting for the deliverance that does not come.'

'It is beautiful,' said Lucien; 'it is the most beautiful thing I ever heard.'

'Where are you going?' asked his hostess, as the young man moved towards the blazing staircase of the east wing.

'I am going to try and save her,' he answered; 'as she has never existed, my death cannot compromise her future existence. I shall go into nothingness, and she, as far as I am concerned, will go into nothingness too; but then she has never been anything else.'

'But your life, your beautiful life?'

'Death in this case is more beautiful.'

The Major started forward.

'I am going too,' he said simply.

'To save Eva?' cried the woman.

'Yes,' he said; 'my little Mildred will not grudge me to a woman who has never existed.'

'How well he reads our sex,' murmured Mrs Gramplain, 'and yet how badly he plays bridge!'

The two men went side by side up the blazing staircase, the slender young figure in the well-fitting dinner-jacket and the thick-set military man in striped pyjamas of an obvious Swan & Edgar pattern. Down in the hall below them stood the woman in her pale wrapper, and the Canon in his wonderfully-hued Albanian-work dressing-gown, looking like the arch-priests of some strange religion presiding at a human sacrifice.

As the rescue-party disappeared into the roaring cavern of smoke and flames, the butler came into the hall, bearing with him one of the Raeburns.

'I think I hear the clanging of the fire-engines, ma'am,' he announced.

Mrs Gramplain continued staring at the spot where the two men had disappeared.

'How stupid of me!' she said presently to the Canon. 'I've just remembered I sent Eva to Exeter to be cleaned. Those two men have lost their lives for nothing.'

'They have certainly lost their lives,' said the Canon.

'The irony of it all,' said Mrs Gramplain, 'the tragic irony of it all!'

'The real irony of the affair lies in the fact that it will be instrumental in working a social revolution of the utmost magnitude,' said the Canon. 'When it becomes known, through the length and breadth of the land, that an army officer and a young ornament of the social world have lost their lives in a country-house fire, started by suffragette incendiarism, the conscience of the country will be aroused, and people will cry out that the price is too heavy to pay. The militants will be in worse odour than ever, but, like the Importunate Widow, they will get their way. Over the charred bodies of Major Boventry and Lucien Wattleskeat the banners of progress and enfranchisement will be carried forward to victory, and the mothers of the nation will henceforth take their part in electing the Mother of Parliaments. England will range herself with Finland and other enlightened countries which have already admitted women to the labours, honours, and responsibilities of the polling-booth. In the early hours of this February morning a candle has been lighted? '

'The fire was caused by an over-heated flue, and not by suffragettes, sir,' interposed the butler.

At that moment a scurry of hoofs and a clanging of bells, together with the hoot of a motor-horn, were heard above the roaring of the flames.

'The fire-brigade!' exclaimed the Canon.

'The fire-brigade and my husband,' said Mrs Gramplain, in her dull level voice; 'it will all begin over again now, the old life, the old unsatisfying weariness, the old monotony; nothing will be changed.'

'Except the east wing,' said the Canon gently.

11

GABRIEL-ERNEST

'There is a wild beast in your woods,' said the artist Cunningham, as he was being driven to the station. It was the only remark he had made during the drive, but as Van Cheele had talked incessantly his companion's silence had not been noticeable.

'A stray fox or two and some resident weasels. Nothing more formidable,' said Van Cheele. The artist said nothing.

'What did you mean about a wild beast?' said Van Cheele later, when they were on the platform.

'Nothing. My imagination. Here is the train,' said Cunningham.

That afternoon Van Cheele went for one of his frequent rambles through his woodland property. He had a stuffed bittern in his study, and knew the names of quite a number of wild flowers, so his aunt had possibly some justification in describing him as a great naturalist. At any rate, he was a great walker. It was his custom to take mental notes of everything he saw during his walks, not so much for the purpose of assisting contemporary science as to provide topics for conversation afterwards. When the bluebells began to show themselves in flower he made a point of informing every one of the fact; the season of the year might have warned his hearers of the likelihood of such an occurrence, but at least they felt that he was being absolutely frank with them.

What Van Cheele saw on this particular afternoon was, however, something far removed from his ordinary range of experience. On a shelf of smooth stone overhanging a deep pool in the hollow of an oak coppice a boy of about sixteen lay asprawl, drying his wet brown limbs luxuriously in the sun. His wet hair, parted by a recent dive, lay close to his head, and his light-brown eyes, so light that there was an almost tigerish gleam in them, were turned towards Van Cheele with a certain lazy watchfulness. It was an unexpected apparition, and Van Cheele found himself engaged in the novel process of thinking before he spoke. Where on earth could this wild-looking boy hail from? The miller's wife had lost a child some two months ago, supposed to have been swept away by the mill-race, but that had been a mere baby, not a half-grown lad.

'What are you doing there?' he demanded.

'Obviously, sunning myself,' replied the boy.

'Where do you live?'

'Here, in these woods.'

'You can't live in the woods,' said Van Cheele.

'They are very nice woods,' said the boy, with a touch of patronage in his voice.

'But where do you sleep at night?'

'I don't sleep at night; that's my busiest time.'

Van Cheele began to have an irritated feeling that he was grappling with a problem that was eluding him.

'What do you feed on?' he asked.

'Flesh,' said the boy, and he pronounced the word with slow relish, as though he were tasting it.

'Flesh! What Flesh?'

'Since it interests you, rabbits, wild-fowl, hares, poultry, lambs in their season, children when I can get any; they're usually too well locked in at night, when I do most of my hunting. It's quite two months since I tasted child-flesh.'

Ignoring the chaffing nature of the last remark Van Cheele tried to draw the boy on the subject of possible poaching operations.

'You're talking rather through your hat when you speak of feeding on hares.' (Considering the nature of the boy's toilet the simile was hardly an apt one.) 'Our hillside hares aren't easily caught.'

'At night I hunt on four feet,' was the somewhat cryptic response.

'I suppose you mean that you hunt with a dog?' hazarded Van Cheele.

The boy rolled slowly over on to his back, and laughed a weird low laugh, that was pleasantly like a chuckle and disagreeably like a snarl.

'I don't fancy any dog would be very anxious for my company, especially at night.'

Van Cheele began to feel that there was something positively uncanny about the strange-eyed, strange-tongued youngster.

'I can't have you staying in these woods,' he declared authoritatively.

'I fancy you'd rather have me here than in your house,' said the boy.

The prospect of this wild, nude animal in Van Cheele's primly ordered house was certainly an alarming one.

'If you don't go. I shall have to make you,' said Van Cheele.

The boy turned like a flash, plunged into the pool, and in a moment had flung his wet and glistening body half-way up the bank where Van Cheele was standing. In an otter the movement would not have been remarkable; in a boy Van Cheele found it sufficiently startling. His foot slipped as he made an involuntarily backward movement, and he found himself almost prostrate on the slippery weed-grown bank, with those tigerish yellow eyes not very far from his own. Almost instinctively he half raised his hand to his throat. The boy laughed again, a laugh in which the snarl had nearly driven out the chuckle, and then, with another of his astonishing lightning movements, plunged out of view into a yielding tangle of weed and fern.

'What an extraordinary wild animal!' said Van Cheele as he picked himself up. And then he recalled Cunningham's remark 'There is a wild beast in your woods.'

Walking slowly homeward, Van Cheele began to turn over in his mind various local occurrences which might be traceable to the existence of this astonishing young savage.

Something had been thinning the game in the woods lately, poultry had been missing from the farms, hares were growing unaccountably scarcer, and complaints had reached him of lambs being carried off bodily from the hills. Was it possible that this wild boy was really hunting the countryside in company with some clever poacher dogs? He had spoken of hunting 'four-footed' by night, but then, again, he had hinted strangely at no dog caring to come near him, 'especially at night'. It was certainly puzzling. And then, as Van Cheele ran his mind over the various depredations that had been committed during the last month or two, he came suddenly to a dead stop, alike in his walk and his speculations. The child missing from the mill two months ago—the accepted theory was that it had tumbled into the mill-race and been swept away; but the mother had always declared she had heard a shriek on the hill side of the house, in the opposite direction from the water. It was unthinkable, of course, but he wished that the boy had not made that uncanny remark about child-flesh eaten two months ago. Such dreadful things should not be said even in fun.

Van Cheele, contrary to his usual wont, did not feel disposed to be communicative about his discovery in the wood. His position as a parish councillor and justice of the peace seemed somehow compromised by the fact that he was harbouring a personality of such doubtful repute on his property; there was even a possibility that a heavy bill of damages for raided lambs and poultry might be laid at his door. At dinner that night he was quite unusually silent.

'Where's your voice gone to?' said his aunt. 'One would think you had seen a wolf.'

Van Cheele, who was not familiar with the old saying, thought the remark rather foolish; if he HAD seen a wolf on his property his tongue would have been extraordinarily busy with the subject.

At breakfast next morning Van Cheele was conscious that his feeling of uneasiness regarding yesterday's episode had not wholly disappeared, and he resolved to go by train to the neighbouring cathedral town, hunt up Cunningham, and learn from him what he had really seen that had prompted the remark about a wild beast in the woods. With this resolution taken, his usual cheerfulness partially returned, and he hummed a bright little melody as he sauntered to the morning-room for his customary cigarette. As he entered the room the melody made way abruptly for a pious invocation. Gracefully asprawl on the ottoman, in an attitude of almost exaggerated repose, was the boy of the woods. He was drier than when Van Cheele had last seen him, but no other alteration was noticeable in his toilet.

'How dare you come here?' asked Van Cheele furiously.

'You told me I was not to stay in the woods,' said the boy calmly.

'But not to come here. Supposing my aunt should see you!'

And with a view to minimising that catastrophe, Van Cheele hastily obscured as much of his unwelcome guest as possible under the folds of a Morning Post. At that moment his aunt entered the room.

'This is a poor boy who has lost his way—and lost his memory. He doesn't know who he is or where he comes from,' explained Van Cheele desperately, glancing apprehensively at the waif's face to see whether he was going to add inconvenient candour to his other savage propensities.

Miss Van Cheele was enormously interested.

'Perhaps his underlinen is marked,' she suggested.

'He seems to have lost most of that, too,' said Van Cheele, making frantic little grabs at the Morning Post to keep it in its place.

A naked homeless child appealed to Miss Van Cheele as warmly as a stray kitten or derelict puppy would have done.

'We must do all we can for him,' she decided, and in a very short time a messenger, dispatched to the rectory, where a page-boy was kept, had returned with a suit of pantry clothes, and the necessary accessories of shirt, shoes, collar, etc. Clothed, clean, and groomed, the boy lost none of his uncanniness in Van Cheele's eyes, but his aunt found him sweet.

'We must call him something till we know who he really is,' she said. 'Gabriel-Ernest, I think; those are nice suitable names.'

Van Cheele agreed, but he privately doubted whether they were being grafted on to a nice suitable child. His misgivings were not diminished by the fact that his staid and elderly spaniel had bolted out of the house at the first incoming of the boy, and now obstinately remained shivering and yapping at the farther end of the orchard, while the canary, usually as vocally industrious as Van Cheele himself, had put itself on an allowance of frightened cheeps. More than ever he was resolved to consult Cunningham without loss of time.

As he drove off to the station his aunt was arranging that Gabriel-Ernest should help her to entertain the infant members of her Sunday-school class at tea that afternoon.

Cunningham was not at first disposed to be communicative.

'My mother died of some brain trouble,' he explained, 'so you will understand why I am averse to dwelling on anything of an impossibly fantastic nature that I may see or think that I have seen.'

'But what DID you see?' persisted Van Cheele.

'What I thought I saw was something so extraordinary that no really sane man could dignify it with the credit of having actually happened. I was standing, the last evening I was with you, half-hidden in the hedgegrowth by the orchard gate, watching the dying glow of the sunset. Suddenly I became aware of a naked boy, a bather from some neighbouring pool, I took him to be, who was standing out on the bare hillside also watching the sunset. His pose was so suggestive of some wild faun of Pagan myth that I instantly wanted to engage him as a model, and in another moment I think I should have hailed him. But just then the sun dipped out of view, and all the orange and pink slid out of the landscape, leaving it cold and grey. And at the same moment an astounding thing happened—the boy vanished too!'

'What! vanished away into nothing?' asked Van Cheele excitedly.

'No; that is the dreadful part of it,' answered the artist; 'on the open hillside where the boy had been standing a second ago, stood a large wolf, blackish in colour, with gleaming fangs and cruel, yellow eyes. You may think—'

But Van Cheele did not stop for anything as futile as thought. Already he was tearing at top speed towards the station. He dismissed the idea of a telegram. 'Gabriel-Ernest is a werewolf' was a hopelessly inadequate effort at conveying the situation, and his aunt would think it was a code message to which he had omitted to give her the key. His one hope was that he might reach home before sundown. The cab which he chartered at the other end of the railway journey bore him with what seemed exasperating slowness along the country roads, which were pink and mauve with the flush of the sinking sun. His aunt was putting away some unfinished jams and cake when he arrived.

'Where is Gabriel-Ernest?' he almost screamed.

'He is taking the little Toop child home,' said his aunt. 'It was getting so late, I thought it wasn't safe to let it go back alone. What a lovely sunset, isn't it?'

But Van Cheele, although not oblivious of the glow in the western sky, did not stay to discuss its beauties. At a speed for which he was scarcely geared he raced along the narrow lane that led to the home of the Toops. On one side ran the swift current of the mill-stream, on the other rose the stretch of bare hillside. A dwindling rim of red sun showed still on the skyline, and the next turning must bring him in view of the ill-assorted couple he was pursuing. Then the colour went suddenly out of things, and a grey light settled itself with a quick shiver over the landscape. Van Cheele heard a shrill wail of fear, and stopped running.

Nothing was ever seen again of the Toop child or Gabriel-Ernest, but the latter's discarded garments were found lying in the road so it was assumed that the child had fallen into the water, and that the boy had stripped and jumped in, in a vain endeavour to save it. Van Cheele and some workmen who were near by at the time testified to having heard a child scream loudly just near the spot where the clothes were found. Mrs Toop, who had eleven other children, was decently resigned to her bereavement, but Miss Van Cheele sincerely mourned her lost foundling. It was on her initiative that a memorial brass was put up in the parish church to 'Gabriel-Ernest, an unknown boy, who bravely sacrificed his life for another.'

Van Cheele gave way to his aunt in most things, but he flatly refused to subscribe to the Gabriel-Ernest memorial.

12

ESMÉ

'All hunting stories are the same,' said Clovis; 'just as all Turf stories are the same, and all—'

'My hunting story isn't a bit like any you've ever heard,' said the Baroness. 'It happened quite a while ago, when I was about twenty-three. I wasn't living apart from my husband then; you see, neither of us could afford to make the other a separate allowance. In spite of everything that proverbs may say, poverty keeps together more homes than it breaks up. But we always hunted with different packs. All this has nothing to do with the story.'

'We haven't arrived at the meet yet. I suppose there was a meet?' said Clovis.

'Of course there was a meet,' said the Baroness; 'all the usual crowd were there, especially Constance Broddle. Constance is one of those strapping florid girls that go so well with autumn scenery or Christmas decorations in church. 'I feel a presentiment that something dreadful is going to happen,' she said to me; 'am I looking pale?'

'She was looking about as pale as a beetroot that has suddenly heard bad news.

"You're looking nicer than usual," I said, 'but that's so easy for you.' Before she had got the right bearings of this remark we had settled down to business; hounds had found a fox lying out in some gorse-bushes.'

'I knew it,' said Clovis; 'in every fox-hunting story that I've ever heard there's been a fox and some gorse-bushes.'

'Constance and I were well mounted,' continued the Baroness serenely, 'and we had no difficulty in keeping ourselves in the first flight, though it was a fairly stiff run. Towards the finish, however, we must have held rather too independent a line, for we lost the hounds, and found ourselves plodding aimlessly along miles away from anywhere. It was fairly exasperating, and my temper was beginning to let itself go by inches, when on pushing our way through an accommodating hedge we were gladdened by the sight of hounds in full cry in a hollow just beneath us.

"There they go,' cried Constance, and then added in a gasp, 'In Heaven's name, what are they hunting?'

'It was certainly no mortal fox. It stood more than twice as high, had a short, ugly head, and an enormous thick neck.

"It's a hyena,' I cried; 'it must have escaped from Lord Pabham's Park.'

'At that moment the hunted beast turned and faced its pursuers, and the hounds (there were only about six couple of them) stood round in a half-circle and looked foolish. Evidently they had broken away from the rest of the pack on the trail of this alien scent, and were not quite sure how to treat their quarry now they had got him.

'The hyena hailed our approach with unmistakable relief and demonstrations of friendliness. It had probably been accustomed to uniform kindness from humans, while its first experience of a pack of hounds had left a bad impression. The hounds looked more than ever embarrassed as their quarry paraded its sudden intimacy with us, and the faint toot of a horn in the distance was seized on as a welcome signal for unobtrusive departure. Constance and I and the hyena were left alone in the gathering twilight.

"What are we to do?' asked Constance.

13

TOBERMORY

It was a chill, rain-washed afternoon of a late August day, that indefinite season when partridges are still in security or cold storage, and there is nothing to hunt—unless one is bounded on the north by the Bristol Channel, in which case one may lawfully gallop after fat red stags. Lady Blemley's house-party was not bounded on the north by the Bristol Channel, hence there was a full gathering of her guests round the tea-table on this particular afternoon. And, in spite of the blankness of the season and the triteness of the occasion, there was no trace in the company of that fatigued restlessness which means a dread of the pianola and a subdued hankering for auction bridge. The undisguised open-mouthed attention of the entire party was fixed on the homely negative personality of Mr Cornelius Appin. Of all her guests, he was the one who had come to Lady Blemley with the vaguest reputation. Some one had said he was 'clever,' and he had got his invitation in the moderate expectation, on the part of his hostess, that some portion at least of his cleverness would be contributed to the general entertainment. Until tea-time that day she had been unable to discover in what direction, if any, his cleverness lay. He was neither a wit nor a croquet champion, a hypnotic force nor a begetter of amateur theatricals. Neither did his exterior suggest the sort of man in whom women are willing to pardon a generous measure of mental deficiency. He had subsided into mere Mr Appin, and the Cornelius seemed a piece of transparent baptismal bluff. And now he was claiming to have launched on the world a discovery beside which the invention of gunpowder, of the printing-press, and of steam locomotion were inconsiderable trifles. Science had made bewildering strides in many directions during recent decades, but this thing seemed to belong to the domain of miracle rather than to scientific achievement.

'And do you really ask us to believe,' Sir Wilfrid was saying, 'that you have discovered a means for instructing animals in the art of human speech, and that dear old Tobermory has proved your first successful pupil?'

'It is a problem at which I have worked for the last seventeen years,' said Mr Appin, 'but only during the last eight or nine months have I been rewarded with glimmerings of success. Of course I have experimented with thousands of animals, but latterly only with cats, those wonderful creatures which have assimilated themselves so marvelously with our civilization while retaining all their highly developed feral instincts. Here and there among cats one comes across an outstanding superior intellect, just as one does among the ruck of human beings, and when I made the acquaintance of Tobermory a week ago I saw at once that I was in contact with a 'Beyond-cat' of extraordinary intelligence. I had gone far along the road to success in recent experiments; with Tobermory, as you call him, I have reached the goal.'

Mr Appin concluded his remarkable statement in a voice which he strove to divest of a triumphant inflection. No one said 'Rats,' though Clovis's lips moved in a monosyllabic contortion, which probably invoked those rodents of disbelief.

'And do you mean to say,' asked Miss Resker, after a slight pause, 'that you have taught Tobermory to say and understand easy sentences of one syllable?'

'My dear Miss Resker,' said the wonder-worker patiently,

'one teaches little children and savages and backward adults in that piecemeal fashion; when one has once solved the problem of making a beginning with an animal of highly developed intelligence one has no need for those halting methods. Tobermory can speak our language with perfect correctness.'

This time Clovis very distinctly said, 'Beyond-rats!' Sir Wilfred was more polite but equally sceptical. 'Hadn't we better have the cat in and judge for ourselves?' suggested Lady Blemley.

Sir Wilfred went in search of the animal, and the company settled themselves down to the languid expectation of witnessing some more or less adroit drawing-room ventriloquism.

In a minute Sir Wilfred was back in the room, his face white beneath its tan and his eyes dilated with excitement.

'By Gad, it's true!'

His agitation was unmistakably genuine, and his hearers started forward in a thrill of wakened interest.

Collapsing into an armchair he continued breathlessly: 'I found him dozing in the smoking-room, and called out to him to come for his tea. He blinked at me in his usual way, and I said, 'Come on, Toby; don't keep us waiting' and, by Gad! he drawled out in a most horribly natural voice that he'd come when he dashed well pleased! I nearly jumped out of my skin!'

Appin had preached to absolutely incredulous hearers; Sir Wilfred's statement carried instant conviction. A Babel-like chorus of startled exclamation arose, amid which the scientist sat mutely enjoying the first fruit of his stupendous discovery.

In the midst of the clamour Tobermory entered the room and made his way with velvet tread and studied unconcern across the group seated round the tea-table. A sudden hush of awkwardness and constraint fell on the company. Somehow there seemed an element of embarrassment in addressing on equal terms a domestic cat of acknowledged mental ability.

'Will you have some milk, Tobermory?' asked Lady Blemley

in a rather strained voice.

'I don't mind if I do,' was the response, couched in a tone of even indifference. A shiver of suppressed excitement went through the listeners, and Lady Blemley might be excused for pouring out the saucerful of milk rather unsteadily.

'I'm afraid I've spilt a good deal of it,' she said apologetically.

'After all, it's not my Axminster,' was Tobermory's rejoinder.

Another silence fell on the group, and then Miss Resker, in her best district-visitor manner, asked if the human language had been difficult to learn. Tobermory looked squarely at her for a moment and then fixed his gaze serenely on the middle distance. It was obvious that boring questions lay outside his scheme of life.

'What do you think of human intelligence?' asked Mavis Pellington lamely.

'Of whose intelligence in particular?' asked Tobermory coldly.

'Oh, well, mine for instance,' said Mavis with a feeble laugh.

'You put me in an embarrassing position,' said Tobermory, whose tone and attitude certainly did not suggest a shred of embarrassment. 'When your inclusion in this house-party was suggested Sir Wilfrid protested that you were the most brainless woman of his acquaintance, and that there was a wide distinction between hospitality and the care of the feeble-minded. Lady Blemley replied that your lack of brain-power was the precise quality which had earned you your invitation, as you were the only person she could think of who might be idiotic enough to buy their old car. You know, the one they call 'The Envy of Sisyphus,' because it goes quite nicely up-hill if you push it.'

Lady Blemley's protestations would have had greater effect if she had not casually suggested to Mavis only that morning that the car in question would be just the thing for her down at her Devonshire home.

Major Barfield plunged in heavily to effect a diversion.

'How about your carryings-on with the tortoise-shell puss up at the stables, eh?'

The moment he had said it every one realized the blunder.

'One does not usually discuss these matters in public,' said Tobermory frigidly. 'From a slight observation of your ways since you've been in this house I should imagine you'd find it inconvenient if I were to shift the conversation to your own little affairs.'

The panic which ensued was not confined to the Major.

'Would you like to go and see if cook has got your dinner ready?' suggested Lady Blemley hurriedly, affecting to ignore the fact that it wanted at least two hours to Tobermory's dinner-time.

'Thanks,' said Tobermory, 'not quite so soon after my tea. I don't want to die of indigestion.'

'Cats have nine lives, you know,' said Sir Wilfred heartily.

'Possibly,' answered Tobermory; 'but only one liver.'

'Adelaide!' said Mrs Cornett, 'Do you mean to encourage that cat to go out and gossip about us in the servants' hall?'

The panic had indeed become general. A narrow ornamental balustrade ran in front of most of the bedroom windows at the Towers, and it was recalled with dismay that this had formed a favourite promenade for Tobermory at all hours, whence he could watch the pigeons—and heaven knew what else besides. If he intended to become reminiscent in his present outspoken strain the effect would be something more than disconcerting. Mrs Cornett, who spent much time at her toilet table, and whose complexion was reputed to be of a nomadic though punctual disposition, looked as ill at ease as the Major. Miss Scrawen, who wrote fiercely sensuous poetry and led a blameless life, merely displayed irritation; if you are methodical and virtuous in private you don't necessarily want everyone to know it. Bertie van Tahn, who was so depraved at 17 that he had long ago given up trying to be any worse, turned a dull shade of gardenia white, but he did not commit the error of dashing out of the room like Odo

Finsberry, a young gentleman who was understood to be reading for the Church and who was possibly disturbed at the thought of scandals he might hear concerning other people.

Clovis had the presence of mind to maintain a composed exterior; privately he was calculating how long it would take to procure a box of fancy mice through the agency of the Exchange and Mart as a species of hush-money. Even in a delicate situation like the present, Agnes Resker could not endure to remain long in the background.

'Why did I ever come down here?' she asked dramatically.

Tobermory immediately accepted the opening.

'Judging by what you said to Mrs Cornett on the croquet-lawn yesterday, you were out of food. You described the Blemleys as the dullest people to stay with that you knew, but said they were clever enough to employ a first-rate cook; otherwise they'd find it difficult to get any one to come down a second time.'

'There's not a word of truth in it! I appeal to Mrs Cornett—' exclaimed the discomfited Agnes.

'Mrs Cornett repeated your remark afterwards to Bertie van Tahn,' continued Tobermory, 'and said, "That woman is a regular Hunger Marcher; she'd go anywhere for four square meals a day,' and Bertie van Tahn said—'

At this point the chronicle mercifully ceased. Tobermory had caught a glimpse of the big yellow tom from the Rectory working his way through the shrubbery towards the stable wing. In a flash he had vanished through the open French window.

With the disappearance of his too brilliant pupil Cornelius Appin found himself beset by a hurricane of bitter upbraiding, anxious inquiry, and frightened entreaty. The responsibility for the situation lay with him, and he must prevent matters from becoming worse. Could Tobermory impart his dangerous gift to other cats? Was the first question he had to answer. It was possible, he replied, that he might have initiated his intimate friend the stable puss into his new accomplishment, but it was unlikely that his teaching could have taken a wider range as yet.

'Then,' said Mrs Cornett, 'Tobermory may be a valuable cat and a great pet; but I'm sure you'll agree, Adelaide, that both he and the stable cat must be done away with without delay.'

'You don't suppose I've enjoyed the last quarter of an hour, do you?' said Lady Blemley bitterly. 'My husband and I are very fond of Tobermory—at least, we were before this horrible accomplishment was infused into him; but now, of course, the only thing is to have him destroyed as soon as possible.'

'We can put some strychnine in the scraps he always gets at dinner-time,' said Sir Wilfred, 'and I will go and drown the stable cat myself. The coachman will be very sore at losing his pet, but I'll say a very catching form of mange has broken out in both cats and we're afraid of it spreading to the kennels.'

'But my great discovery!' expostulated Mr Appin; 'after all my years of research and experiment—'

'You can go and experiment on the short-horns at the farm, who are under proper control,' said MrsCornett, 'or the elephants at the Zoological Gardens. They're said to be highly intelligent, and they have this recommendation, that they don't come creeping about our bedrooms and under chairs, and so forth.'

An archangel ecstatically proclaiming the Millennium, and then finding that it clashed unpardonably with Henley and would have to be indefinitely postponed, could hardly have felt more crestfallen than Cornelius Appin at the reception of his wonderful achievement. Public opinion, however, was against him—in fact, had the general voice been consulted on the subject it is probable that a strong minority vote would have been in favour of including him in the strychnine diet.

Defective train arrangements and a nervous desire to see matters brought to a finish prevented an immediate dispersal of the party, but dinner that evening was not a social success. Sir

Wilfred had had rather a trying time with the stable cat and subsequently with the coachman. Agnes Resker ostentatiously limited her repast to a morsel of dry toast, which she bit as though it were a personal enemy; while Mavis Pellington maintained a vindictive silence throughout the meal. Lady Blemley kept up a flow of what she hoped was conversation, but her attention was fixed on the doorway. A plateful of carefully dosed fish scraps was in readiness on the sideboard, but the sweets and savoury and dessert went their way, and no Tobermory appeared in the dining-room or kitchen.

The sepulchral dinner was cheerful compared with the subsequent vigil in the smoking-room. Eating and drinking had at least supplied a distraction and cloak to the prevailing embarrassment. Bridge was out of the question in the general tension of nerves and tempers, and after Odo Finsberry had given a lugubrious rendering of 'Melisande in the Wood' to a frigid audience, music was tacitly avoided. At eleven the servants went to bed, announcing that the small window in the pantry had been left open as usual for Tobermory's private use. The guests read steadily through the current batch of magazines, and fell back gradually on the 'Badminton Library' and bound volumes of Punch. Lady Blemley made periodic visits to the pantry, returning each time with an expression of listless depression which forestalled questioning. At two o'clock Clovis broke the dominating silence.

'He won't turn up tonight. He's probably in the local newspaper office at the present moment, dictating the first installment of his reminiscences. Lady What's-her-name's book won't be in it. It will be the event of the day.'

Having made this contribution to the general cheerfulness, Clovis went to bed. At long intervals the various members of the house-party followed his example.

The servants taking round the early tea made a uniform announcement in reply to a uniform question.

Tobermory had not returned.

Breakfast was, if anything, a more unpleasant function than dinner had been, but before its conclusion the situation was relieved. Tobermory's corpse was brought in from the shrubbery, where a gardener had just discovered it. From the bites on his throat and the yellow fur which coated his claws it was evident that he had fallen in unequal combat with the big Tom from the Rectory.

By midday most of the guests had quitted the Towers, and after lunch Lady Blemley had sufficiently recovered her spirits to write an extremely nasty letter to the Rectory about the loss of her valuable pet.

Tobermory had been Appin's one successful pupil, and he was destined to have no successor. A few weeks later an elephant in the Dresden Zoological Garden, which had shown no previous signs of irritability, broke loose and killed an Englishman who had apparently been teasing it. The victim's name was variously reported in the papers as Oppin and Eppelin, but his front name was faithfully rendered Cornelius.

'If he was trying German irregular verbs on the poor beast,' said Clovis, 'he deserved all he got.'

14

THE BULL

Tom Yorkfield had always regarded his half-brother, Laurence, with a lazy instinct of dislike, toned down, as years went on, to a tolerant feeling of indifference. There was nothing very tangible to dislike him for; he was just a blood-relation, with whom Tom had no single taste or interest in common, and with whom, at the same time, he had had no occasion for quarrel. Laurence had left the farm early in life, and had lived for a few years on a small sum of money left him by his mother; he had taken up painting as a profession, and was reported to be doing fairly well at it, well enough, at any rate, to keep body and soul together. He specialised in painting animals, and he was successful in finding a certain number of people to buy his pictures. Tom felt a comforting sense of assured superiority in contrasting his position with that of his half-brother; Laurence was an artist-chap, just that and nothing more, though you might make it sound more important by calling an animal painter; Tom was a farmer, not in a very big way, it was true, but the Helsery farm had been in the family for some generations, and it had a good reputation for the stock raised on it. Tom had done his best, with the little capital at his command, to maintain and improve the standard of his small herd of cattle, and in Clover Fairy he had bred a bull which was something rather better than any that his immediate neighbours could show. It would not have made a sensation in the judging-ring at an important cattle show, but it was as vigorous, shapely, and healthy a young animal as any small practical farmer could wish to possess. At the King's Head on market days Clover Fairy was very highly spoken of, and Yorkfield used to declare that he would not part with him for a hundred pounds; a hundred pounds is a lot of money in the small farming line, and probably anything over eighty would have tempted him.

It was with some especial pleasure that Tom took advantage of one of Laurence's rare visits to the farm to lead him down to the enclosure where Clover Fairy kept solitary state—the grass widower of a grazing harem. Tom felt some of his old dislike for his half- brother reviving; the artist was becoming more languid in his manner, more unsuitably turned-out in attire, and he seemed inclined to impart a slightly patronising tone to his conversation. He took no heed of a flourishing potato crop, but waxed enthusiastic over a clump of yellow-flowering weed that stood in a corner by a gateway, which was rather galling to the owner of a really very well weeded farm; again, when he might have been duly complimentary about a group of fat, black-faced lambs, that simply cried aloud for admiration, he became eloquent over the foliage tints of an oak copse on the hill opposite. But now he was being taken to inspect the crowning pride and glory of Helsery; however grudging he might be in his praises, however backward and niggardly with his congratulations, he would have to see and acknowledge the many excellences of that redoubtable animal. Some weeks ago, while on a business journey to Taunton, Tom had been invited by his half-brother to visit a studio in that town, where Laurence was exhibiting one of his pictures, a large canvas representing a bull standing knee-deep in some marshy ground; it had been good of its kind, no doubt, and Laurence had seemed inordinately pleased with it; 'the best thing I've done yet,' he had said over and over again, and Tom had generously agreed that it was fairly life-like. Now, the man of pigments was going to be shown a real picture, a living model of strength and comeliness, a thing to feast the eyes on, a picture that exhibited new pose and action with every shifting minute, instead of standing glued into one unvarying attitude between the four walls of a frame. Tom unfastened a stout wooden door and led the way into a straw-bedded yard.

'Is he quiet?' asked the artist, as a young bull with a curly red coat came inquiringly towards them.

'He's playful at times,' said Tom, leaving his half-brother to wonder whether the bull's ideas of play were of the catch-as-catch-can order. Laurence made one or two perfunctory comments on the animal's appearance and asked a question or so as to his age and such-like details; then he coolly turned the talk into another channel.

'Do you remember the picture I showed you at Taunton?' he asked.

'Yes,' grunted Tom; 'a white-faced bull standing in some slush. Don't admire those Herefords much myself; bulky-looking brutes, don't seem to have much life in them. Daresay they're easier to paint that way; now, this young beggar is on the move all the time, aren't you, Fairy?'

'I've sold that picture,' said Laurence, with considerable complacency in his voice.

'Have you?' said Tom; 'glad to hear it, I'm sure. Hope you're pleased with what you've got for it.'

'I got three hundred pounds for it,' said Laurence.

Tom turned towards him with a slowly rising flush of anger in his face. Three hundred pounds! Under the most favourable market conditions that he could imagine his prized Clover Fairy would hardly fetch a hundred, yet here was a piece of varnished canvas, painted by his half-brother, selling for three times that sum. It was a cruel insult that went home with all the more force because it emphasised the triumph of the patronising, self-satisfied Laurence. The young farmer had meant to put his relative just a little out of conceit with himself by displaying the jewel of his possessions, and now the tables were turned, and his valued beast was made to look cheap and insignificant beside the price paid for a mere picture. It was so monstrously unjust; the painting would never be anything more than a dexterous piece of counterfeit life, while Clover Fairy was the real thing, a monarch in his little world, a personality in the countryside. After he was dead, even, he would still be something of a personality; his descendants would graze in those valley meadows and hillside pastures, they would fill stall and byre and milking-shed, their good red coats would speckle the landscape and crowd the market-place; men would note a promising heifer or a well-proportioned steer, and say: 'Ah, that one comes of good old Clover Fairy's stock.' All that time the picture would be hanging, lifeless and unchanging, beneath its dust and varnish, a chattel that ceased to mean anything if you chose to turn it with its back to the wall. These thoughts chased themselves angrily through Tom Yorkfield's mind, but he could not put them into words. When he gave tongue to his feelings he put matters bluntly and harshly.

'Some soft-witted fools may like to throw away three hundred pounds on a bit of paintwork; can't say as I envy them their taste. I'd rather have the real thing than a picture of it.'

He nodded towards the young bull, that was alternately staring at them with nose held high and lowering its horns with a half-playful, half-impatient shake of the head.

Laurence laughed a laugh of irritating, indulgent amusement.

'I don't think the purchaser of my bit of paintwork, as you call it, need worry about having thrown his money away. As I get to be better known and recognised my pictures will go up in value. That particular one will probably fetch four hundred in a sale-room five or six years hence; pictures aren't a bad investment if you know enough to pick out the work of the right men. Now you can't say your precious bull is going to get more valuable the longer you keep him; he'll have his little day, and then, if you go on keeping him, he'll come down at last to a few shillingsworth of hoofs and hide, just at a time, perhaps, when my bull is being bought for a big sum for some important picture gallery.'

It was too much. The united force of truth and slander and insult put over heavy a strain on Tom Yorkfield's powers of restraint. In his right hand he held a useful oak cudgel, with his left he made a grab at the loose collar of Laurence's canary-coloured silk shirt. Laurence was not a fighting man; the fear of physical violence threw him off his balance as completely as overmastering indignation had thrown Tom off his, and thus it came to pass that Clover Fairy was regaled with the unprecedented sight of a human being scudding and squawking across the enclosure, like the hen that would persist in trying to establish a nesting-place in the manger. In another crowded happy moment the bull was trying to jerk Laurence over his left shoulder, to prod him in the ribs while still in the air, and to kneel on him when he reached the ground. It was only the vigorous intervention of Tom that induced him to relinquish the last item of his programme.

Tom devotedly and ungrudgingly nursed his half brother to a complete recovery from his injuries, which consisted of nothing more serious than a dislocated shoulder, a broken rib or two, and a little nervous prostration. After all, there was no further occasion for rancour in the young farmer's mind; Laurence's bull might sell for three hundred, or for six hundred, and be admired by thousands in some big picture gallery, but it would never toss a man over one shoulder and catch him a jab in the ribs before he had fallen on the other side. That was Clover Fairy's noteworthy achievement, which could never be taken away from him.

Laurence continues to be popular as an animal artist, but his subjects are always kittens or fawns or lambkins—never bulls.

15

THE INTERLOPERS

In a forest of mixed growth somewhere on the eastern spurs of the Karpathians, a man stood one winter night watching and listening, as though he waited for some beast of the woods to come within the range of his vision, and, later, of his rifle. But the game for whose presence he kept so keen an outlook was none that figured in the sportsman's calendar as lawful and proper for the chase; Ulrich von Gradwitz patrolled the dark forest in quest of a human enemy.

The forest lands of Gradwitz were of wide extent and well stocked with game; the narrow strip of precipitous woodland that lay on its outskirt was not remarkable for the game it harboured or the shooting it afforded, but it was the most jealously guarded of all its owner's territorial possessions. A famous law suit, in the days of his grandfather, had wrested it from the illegal possession of a neighbouring family of petty landowners; the dispossessed party had never acquiesced in the judgment of the Courts, and a long series of poaching affrays and similar scandals had embittered the relationships between the families for three generations. The neighbour feud had grown into a personal one since Ulrich had come to be head of his family; if there was a man in the world whom he detested and wished ill to it was Georg Znaeym, the inheritor of the quarrel and the tireless game-snatcher and raider of the disputed border-forest. The feud might, perhaps, have died down or been compromised if the personal ill-will of the two men had not stood in the way; as boys they had thirsted for one another's blood, as men each prayed that misfortune might fall on the other, and this wind-scourged winter night Ulrich had banded together his foresters to watch the dark forest, not in quest of four-footed quarry, but to keep a look-out for the prowling thieves whom he suspected of being afoot from across the land boundary. The roebuck, which usually kept in the sheltered hollows during a storm-wind, were running like driven things to-night, and there was movement and unrest among the creatures that were wont to sleep through the dark hours. Assuredly there was a disturbing element in the forest, and Ulrich could guess the quarter from whence it came.

He strayed away by himself from the watchers whom he had placed in ambush on the crest of the hill, and wandered far down the steep slopes amid the wild tangle of undergrowth, peering through the tree trunks and listening through the whistling and skirling of the wind and the restless beating of the branches for sight and sound of the marauders. If only on this wild night, in this dark, lone spot, he might come across Georg Znaeym, man to man, with none to witness—that was the wish that was uppermost in his thoughts. And as he stepped round the trunk of a huge beech he came face to face with the man he sought.

The two enemies stood glaring at one another for a long silent moment. Each had a rifle in his hand, each had hate in his heart and murder uppermost in his mind. The chance had come to give full play to the passions of a lifetime. But a man who has been brought up under the code of a restraining civilisation cannot easily nerve himself to shoot down his neighbour in cold blood and without a word spoken, except for an offence against his hearth and honour. And before the moment of hesitation had given way to action a deed of Nature's own violence overwhelmed them both. A fierce shriek of the storm had been answered by a splitting crash over their heads, and ere they could leap aside a mass of falling beech tree had thundered down on them. Ulrich von Gradwitz found himself stretched on the ground, one arm numb beneath him and the other held almost as helplessly in a tight tangle of forked branches, while both legs were pinned beneath the fallen mass. His heavy shooting-boots had saved his feet from being crushed to pieces, but if his fractures were not as serious as they might have been, at least it was evident that he could not move from his present position till some one came to release him. The descending twig had slashed the skin of his face, and he had to wink away some drops of blood from his eyelashes before he could take in a general view of the disaster. At his side, so near that under ordinary circumstances he could almost have touched him, lay Georg Znaeym, alive and struggling, but obviously as helplessly pinioned down as himself. All round them lay a thick-strewn wreckage of splintered branches and broken twigs.

Relief at being alive and exasperation at his captive plight brought a strange medley of pious thank-offerings and sharp curses to Ulrich's lips. Georg, who was early blinded with the blood which trickled across his eyes, stopped his struggling for a moment to listen, and then gave a short, snarling laugh.

'So you're not killed, as you ought to be, but you're caught, anyway,' he cried; 'caught fast. Ho, what a jest, Ulrich von Gradwitz snared in his stolen forest. There's real justice for you!'

And he laughed again, mockingly and savagely.

'I'm caught in my own forest-land,' retorted Ulrich. 'When my men come to release us you will wish, perhaps, that you were in a better plight than caught poaching on a neighbour's land, shame on you.'

Georg was silent for a moment; then he answered quietly:

'Are you sure that your men will find much to release? I have men, too, in the forest tonight, close behind me, and THEY will be here first and do the releasing. When they drag me out from under these damned branches it won't need much clumsiness on their part to roll this mass of trunk right over on the top of you. Your men will find you dead under a fallen beech tree. For form's sake I shall send my condolences to your family.'

'It is a useful hint,' said Ulrich fiercely. 'My men had orders to follow in ten minutes time, seven of which must have gone by already, and when they get me out—I will remember the hint. Only as you will have met your death poaching on my lands I don't think I can decently send any message of condolence to your family.'

'Good,' snarled Georg, 'good. We fight this quarrel out to the death, you and I and our foresters, with no cursed interlopers to come between us. Death and damnation to you, Ulrich von Gradwitz.'

'The same to you, Georg Znaeym, forest-thief, game-snatcher.'

Both men spoke with the bitterness of possible defeat before them, for each knew that it might be long before his men would seek him out or find him; it was a bare matter of chance which party would arrive first on the scene.

Both had now given up the useless struggle to free themselves from the mass of wood that held them down; Ulrich limited his endeavours to an effort to bring his one partially free arm near enough to his outer coat-pocket to draw out his wine-flask. Even when he had accomplished that operation it was long before he could manage the unscrewing of the stopper or get any of the liquid down his throat. But what a Heaven-sent draught it seemed! It was an open winter, and little snow had fallen as yet, hence the captives suffered less from the cold than might have been the case at that season of the year; nevertheless, the wine was warming and reviving to the wounded man, and he looked across with something like a throb of pity to where his enemy lay, just keeping the groans of pain and weariness from crossing his lips.

'Could you reach this flask if I threw it over to you?' asked Ulrich suddenly; 'there is good wine in it, and one may as well be as comfortable as one can. Let us drink, even if to-night one of us dies.'

'No, I can scarcely see anything; there is so much blood caked round my eyes,' said Georg, 'and in any case I don't drink wine with an enemy.'

Ulrich was silent for a few minutes, and lay listening to the weary screeching of the wind. An idea was slowly forming and growing in his brain, an idea that gained strength every time that he looked across at the man who was fighting so grimly against pain and exhaustion. In the pain and languor that Ulrich himself was feeling the old fierce hatred seemed to be dying down.

'Neighbour,' he said presently, 'do as you please if your men come first. It was a fair compact. But as for me, I've changed my mind. If my men are the first to come you shall be the first to be helped, as though you were my guest. We have quarrelled like devils all our lives over this stupid strip of forest, where the trees can't even stand upright in a breath of wind. Lying here tonight thinking, I've come to think we've been rather fools; there are better things in life than getting the better of a boundary dispute. Neighbour, if you will help me to bury the old quarrel I—I will ask you to be my friend.'

Georg Znaeym was silent for so long that Ulrich thought, perhaps, he had fainted with the pain of his injuries. Then he spoke slowly and in jerks.

'How the whole region would stare and gabble if we rode into the market-square together. No one living can remember seeing a Znaeym and a von Gradwitz talking to one another in friendship. And what peace there would be among the forester folk if we ended our feud to-night. And if we choose to make peace among our people there is none other to interfere, no interlopers from outside... You would come and keep the Sylvester night beneath my roof, and I would come and feast on some high day at your castle... I would never fire a shot on your land, save when you invited me as a guest; and you should come and shoot with me down in the marshes where the wildfowl are. In all the countryside there are none that could hinder if we willed to make peace. I never thought to have wanted to do other than hate you all my life, but I think I have changed my mind about things too, this last half-hour. And you offered me your wineflask... Ulrich von Gradwitz, I will be your friend.'

For a space both men were silent, turning over in their minds the wonderful changes that this dramatic reconciliation would bring about. In the cold, gloomy forest, with the wind tearing in fitful gusts through the naked branches and whistling round the tree-trunks, they lay and waited for the help that would now bring release and succour to both parties. And each prayed a private prayer that his men might be the first to arrive, so that he might be the first to show honourable attention to the enemy that had become a friend.

Presently, as the wind dropped for a moment, Ulrich broke silence.

'Let's shout for help,' he said; he said; 'in this lull our voices may carry a little way.'

'They won't carry far through the trees and undergrowth,' said Georg, 'but we can try. Together, then.'

The two raised their voices in a prolonged hunting call.

'Together again,' said Ulrich a few minutes later, after listening in vain for an answering halloo.

'I heard nothing but the pestilential wind,' said Georg hoarsely.

There was silence again for some minutes, and then Ulrich gave a joyful cry.

'I can see figures coming through the wood. They are following in the way I came down the hillside.'

Both men raised their voices in as loud a shout as they could muster.

'They hear us! They've stopped. Now they see us. They're running down the hill towards us,' cried Ulrich.

'How many of them are there?' asked Georg.

'I can't see distinctly,' said Ulrich; 'nine or ten,'

'Then they are yours,' said Georg; 'I had only seven out with me.'

'They are making all the speed they can, brave lads,' said Ulrich gladly.

'Are they your men?' asked Georg. 'Are they your men?' he repeated impatiently as Ulrich did not answer.

'No,' said Ulrich with a laugh, the idiotic chattering laugh of a man unstrung with hideous fear.

'Who are they?' asked Georg quickly, straining his eyes to see what the other would gladly not have seen.

'Wolves.'

16

THE SCHARTZ-METTERKLUME
METHOD

Lady Carlotta stepped out on to the platform of the small wayside station and took a turn or two up and down its uninteresting length, to kill time till the train should be pleased to proceed on its way. Then, in the roadway beyond, she saw a horse struggling with a more than ample load, and a carter of the sort that seems to bear a sullen hatred against the animal that helps him to earn a living. Lady Carlotta promptly betook her to the roadway, and put rather a different complexion on the struggle. Certain of her acquaintances were wont to give her plentiful admonition as to the undesirability of interfering on behalf of a distressed animal, such interference being 'none of her business'. Only once had she put the doctrine of non-interference into practice, when one of its most eloquent exponents had been besieged for nearly three hours in a small and extremely uncomfortable may-tree by an angry boar-pig, while Lady Carlotta, on the other side of the fence, had proceeded with the water-colour sketch she was engaged on, and refused to interfere between the boar and his prisoner. It is to be feared that she lost the friendship of the ultimately rescued lady. On this occasion she merely lost the train, which gave way to the first sign of impatience it had shown throughout the journey, and steamed off without her. She bore the desertion with philosophical indifference; her friends and relations were thoroughly well used to the fact of her luggage arriving without her. She wired a vague non-committal message to her destination to say that she was coming on 'by another train'. Before she had time to think what her next move might be she was confronted by an imposingly attired lady, who seemed to be taking a prolonged mental inventory of her clothes and looks.

'You must be Miss Hope, the governess I've come to meet,' said the apparition, in a tone that admitted of very little argument.

'Very well, if I must I must,' said Lady Carlotta to herself with dangerous meekness.

'I am Mrs Quabarl,' continued the lady; 'and where, pray, is your luggage?'

'It's gone astray,' said the alleged governess, falling in with the excellent rule of life that the absent are always to blame; the luggage had, in point of fact, behaved with perfect correctitude. 'I've just telegraphed about it,' she added, with a nearer approach to truth.

'How provoking,' said Mrs Quabarl; 'these railway companies are so careless. However, my maid can lend you things for the night,' and she led the way to her car.

During the drive to the Quabarl mansion Lady Carlotta was impressively introduced to the nature of the charge that had been thrust upon her; she learned that Claude and Wilfrid were delicate, sensitive young people, that Irene had the artistic temperament highly developed, and that Viola was something or other else of a mould equally commonplace among children of that class and type in the twentieth century.

'I wish them not only to be TAUGHT,' said Mrs Quabarl, 'but INTERESTED in what they learn. In their history lessons, for instance, you must try to make them feel that they are being introduced to the life-stories of men and women who really lived, not merely committing a mass of names and dates to memory. French, of course, I shall expect you to talk at meal-times several days in the week.'

'I shall talk French four days of the week and Russian in the remaining three.'

'Russian? My dear Miss Hope, no one in the house speaks or understands Russian.'

'That will not embarrass me in the least,' said Lady Carlotta coldly.

Mrs Quabarl, to use a colloquial expression, was knocked off her perch. She was one of those imperfectly self-assured individuals who are magnificent and autocratic as long as they are not seriously opposed. The least show of unexpected resistance goes a long way towards rendering them cowed and apologetic. When the new governess failed to express wondering admiration of the large newly-purchased and expensive car, and lightly alluded to the superior advantages of one or two makes which had just been put on the market, the discomfiture of her patroness became almost abject. Her feelings were those which might have animated a general of ancient warfaring days, on beholding his heaviest battle-elephant ignominiously driven off the field by slingers and javelin throwers.

At dinner that evening, although reinforced by her husband, who usually duplicated her opinions and lent her moral support generally, Mrs Quabarl regained none of her lost ground. The governess not only helped herself well and truly to wine, but held forth with considerable show of critical knowledge on various vintage matters, concerning which the Quabarls were in no wise able to pose as authorities. Previous governesses had limited their conversation on the wine topic to a respectful and doubtless sincere expression of a preference for water. When this one went as far as to recommend a wine firm in whose hands you could not go very far wrong Mrs Quabarl thought it time to turn the conversation into more usual channels.

'We got very satisfactory references about you from Canon Teep,' she observed; 'a very estimable man, I should think.'

'Drinks like a fish and beats his wife, otherwise a very lovable character,' said the governess imperturbably.

'MY DEAR Miss Hope! I trust you are exaggerating,' exclaimed the Quabarls in unison.

'One must in justice admit that there is some provocation,' continued the romancer. 'Mrs Teep is quite the most irritating bridge-player that I have ever sat down with; her leads and declarations would condone a certain amount of brutality in her partner, but to souse her with the contents of the only soda-water syphon in the house on a Sunday afternoon, when one couldn't get another, argues an indifference to the comfort of others which I cannot altogether overlook. You may think me hasty in my judgments, but it was practically on account of the syphon incident that I left.'

'We will talk of this some other time,' said Mrs Quabarl hastily.

'I shall never allude to it again,' said the governess with decision.

Mr Quabarl made a welcome diversion by asking what studies the new instructress proposed to inaugurate on the morrow.

'History to begin with,' she informed him.

'Ah, history,' he observed sagely; 'now in teaching them history you must take care to interest them in what they learn. You must make them feel that they are being introduced to the life-stories of men and women who really lived—'

'I've told her all that,' interposed Mrs Quabarl.

'I teach history on the Schartz-Metterklume method,' said the governess loftily.

'Ah, yes,' said her listeners, thinking it expedient to assume an acquaintance at least with the name.

'What are you children doing out here?' demanded Mrs

Quabarl the next morning, on finding Irene sitting rather glumly at the head of the stairs, while her sister was perched in an attitude of depressed discomfort on the window-seat behind her, with a wolf-skin rug almost covering her.

'We are having a history lesson,' came the unexpected reply. 'I am supposed to be Rome, and Viola up there is the she-wolf; not a real wolf, but the figure of one that the Romans used to set store by—I forget why. Claude and Wilfrid have gone to fetch the shabby women.'

'The shabby women?'

'Yes, they've got to carry them off. They didn't want to, but Miss Hope got one of father's fives-bats and said she'd give them a number nine spanking if they didn't, so they've gone to do it.'

A loud, angry screaming from the direction of the lawn drew Mrs Quabarl thither in hot haste, fearful lest the threatened castigation might even now be in process of infliction. The outcry, however, came principally from the two small daughters of the lodge-keeper, who were being hauled and pushed towards the house by the panting and dishevelled Claude and Wilfrid, whose task was rendered even more arduous by the incessant, if not very effectual, attacks of the captured maidens' small brother. The governess, fives-bat in hand, sat negligently on the stone balustrade, presiding over the scene with the cold impartiality of a Goddess of Battles. A furious and repeated chorus of 'I'll tell muvver' rose from the lodge-children, but the lodge-mother, who was hard of hearing, was for the moment immersed in the preoccupation of her washtub.

After an apprehensive glance in the direction of the lodge (the good woman was gifted with the highly militant temper which is sometimes the privilege of deafness) Mrs Quabarl flew indignantly to the rescue of the struggling captives.

'Wilfrid! Claude! Let those children go at once. Miss Hope, what on earth is the meaning of this scene?'

'Early Roman history; the Sabine Women, don't you know? It's the Schartz-Metterklume method to make children understand history by acting it themselves; fixes it in their memory, you know. Of course, if, thanks to your interference, your boys go through life thinking that the Sabine women ultimately escaped, I really cannot be held responsible.'

'You may be very clever and modern, Miss Hope,' said Mrs Quabarl firmly, 'but I should like you to leave here by the next train. Your luggage will be sent after you as soon as it arrives.'

'I'm not certain exactly where I shall be for the next few days,' said the dismissed instructress of youth; 'you might keep my luggage till I wire my address. There are only a couple of trunks and some golf-clubs and a leopard cub.'

'A leopard cub!' gasped Mrs Quabarl. Even in her departure this extraordinary person seemed destined to leave a trail of embarrassment behind her.

'Well, it's rather left off being a cub; it's more than half-grown, you know. A fowl every day and a rabbit on Sundays is what it usually gets. Raw beef makes it too excitable. Don't trouble about getting the car for me, I'm rather inclined for a walk.'

And Lady Carlotta strode out of the Quabarl horizon.

The advent of the genuine Miss Hope, who had made a mistake as to the day on which she was due to arrive, caused a turmoil which that good lady was quite unused to inspiring. Obviously the Quabarl family had been woefully befooled, but a certain amount of relief came with the knowledge.

'How tiresome for you, dear Carlotta,' said her hostess, when the overdue guest ultimately arrived; 'how very tiresome losing your train and having to stop overnight in a strange place.'

'Oh dear, no,' said Lady Carlotta; 'not at all tiresome—for me.'

17

THE MATCH-MAKER

The grill-room clock struck eleven with the respectful unobtrusiveness of one whose mission in life is to be ignored. When the flight of time should really have rendered abstinence and migration imperative, the lighting apparatus would signal the fact in the usual way.

Six minutes later Clovis approached the supper-table, in the blessed expectancy of one who has dined sketchily and long ago.

'I'm starving,' he announced, making an effort to sit down gracefully and read the menu at the same time.

'So I gathered;' said his host, 'from the fact that you were nearly punctual. I ought to have told you that I'm a Food Reformer. I've ordered two bowls of bread-and-milk and some health biscuits. I hope you don't mind.'

Clovis pretended afterwards that he didn't go white above the collar-line for the fraction of a second.

'All the same,' he said, 'you ought not to joke about such things. There really are such people. I've known people who've met them. To think of all the adorable things there are to eat in the world, and then to go through life munching sawdust and being proud of it.'

'They're like the Flagellants of the Middle Ages, who went about mortifying themselves.'

'They had some excuse,' said Clovis. 'They did it to save their immortal souls, didn't they? You needn't tell me that a man who doesn't love oysters and asparagus and good wines has got a soul, or a stomach either. He's simply got the instinct for being unhappy highly developed.'

Clovis relapsed for a few golden moments into tender intimacies with a succession of rapidly disappearing oysters.

'I think oysters are more beautiful than any religion,' he resumed presently. 'They not only forgive our unkindness to them; they justify it, they incite us to go on being perfectly horrid to them. Once they arrive at the supper table they seem to enter thoroughly into the spirit of the thing. There's nothing in Christianity or Buddhism that quite matches the sympathetic unselfishness of an oyster. Do you like my new waistcoat? I'm wearing it for the first time tonight.'

'It looks like a great many others you've had lately, only worse. New dinner waistcoats are becoming a habit with you.'

'They say one always pays for the excesses of one's youth; mercifully that isn't true about one's clothes. My mother is thinking of getting married.'

'Again!'

'It's the first time.'

'Of course, you ought to know. I was under the impression that she'd been married once or twice at least.'

'Three times, to be mathematically exact. I meant that it was the first time she'd thought about getting married; the other times she did it without thinking. As a matter of fact, it's really I who am doing the thinking for her in this case. You see, it's quite two years since her last husband died.'

'You evidently think that brevity is the soul of widowhood.'

'Well, it struck me that she was getting moped, and beginning to settle down, which wouldn't suit her a bit. The first symptom that I noticed was when she began to complain that we were living beyond our income. All decent people live beyond their incomes nowadays, and those who aren't respectable live beyond other peoples. A few gifted individuals manage to do both.'

'It's hardly so much a gift as an industry.'

'The crisis came,' returned Clovis, 'when she suddenly started the theory that late hours were bad for one, and wanted me to be in by one o'clock every night. Imagine that sort of thing for me, who was eighteen on my last birthday.'

'On your last two birthdays, to be mathematically exact.'

'Oh, well, that's not my fault. I'm not going to arrive at nineteen as long as my mother remains at thirty-seven. One must have some regard for appearances.'

'Perhaps your mother would age a little in the process of settling down.'

'That's the last thing she'd think of. Feminine reformations always start in on the failings of other people. That's why I was so keen on the husband idea.'

'Did you go as far as to select the gentleman, or did you merely throw out a general idea, and trust to the force of suggestion?'

'If one wants a thing done in a hurry one must see to it oneself. I found a military Johnny hanging round on a loose end at the club, and took him home to lunch once or twice. He'd spent most of his life on the Indian frontier, building roads, and relieving famines and minimizing earthquakes, and all that sort of thing that one does do on frontiers. He could talk sense to a peevish cobra in fifteen native languages, and probably knew what to do if you found a rogue elephant on your croquet-lawn; but he was shy and diffident with women. I told my mother privately that he was an absolute woman-hater; so, of course, she laid herself out to flirt all she knew, which isn't a little.'

'And was the gentleman responsive?'

'I hear he told some one at the club that he was looking out for a Colonial job, with plenty of hard work, for a young friend of his, so I gather that he has some idea of marrying into the family.'

'You seem destined to be the victim of the reformation, after all.'

Clovis wiped the trace of Turkish coffee and the beginnings of a smile from his lips, and slowly lowered his dexter eyelid. Which, being interpreted, probably meant, 'I DON'T think!'

18

HERMANN THE IRASCIBLE—
A STORY OF THE GREAT WEEP

It was in the second decade of the twentieth century, after the Great Plague had devastated England, that Hermann the Irascible, nicknamed also the Wise, sat on the British throne. The Mortal Sickness had swept away the entire Royal Family, unto the third and fourth generations, and thus it came to pass that Hermann the Fourteenth of Saxe-Drachsen-Wachtelstein, who had stood thirtieth in the order of succession, found himself one day ruler of the British dominions within and beyond the seas. He was one of the unexpected things that happen in politics, and he happened with great thoroughness. In many ways he was the most progressive monarch who had sat on an important throne; before people knew where they were, they were somewhere else. Even his Ministers, progressive though they were by tradition, found it difficult to keep pace with his legislative suggestions.

'As a matter of fact,' admitted the Prime Minister, 'we are hampered by these votes-for-women creatures; they disturb our meetings throughout the country, and they try to turn Downing Street into a sort of political picnic-ground.'

'They must be dealt with,' said Hermann.

'Dealt with,' said the Prime Minister; 'exactly, just so; but how?'

'I will draft you a Bill,' said the King, sitting down at his typewriting machine, 'enacting that women shall vote at all future elections. Shall vote, you observe; or, to put it plainer, must. Voting will remain optional, as before, for male electors; but every woman between the ages of twenty-one and seventy will be obliged to vote, not only at elections for Parliament, county councils, district boards, parish councils, and municipalities, but for coroners, school inspectors, churchwardens, curators of museums, sanitary authorities, police-court interpreters, swimming-bath instructors, contractors, choir-masters, market superintendents, art-school teachers, cathedral vergers, and other local functionaries whose names I will add as they occur to me. All these offices will become elective, and failure to vote at any election falling within her area of residence will involve the female elector in a penalty of £10. Absence, unsupported by an adequate medical certificate, will not be accepted as an excuse. Pass this Bill through the two Houses of Parliament and bring it to me for signature the day after to-morrow.'

From the very outset the Compulsory Female Franchise produced little or no elation even in circles which had been loudest in demanding the vote. The bulk of the women of the country had been indifferent or hostile to the franchise agitation, and the most fanatical Suffragettes began to wonder what they had found so attractive in the prospect of putting ballot-papers into a box. In the country districts the task of carrying out the provisions of the new Act was irksome enough; in the towns and cities it became an incubus. There seemed no end to the elections. Laundresses and seamstresses had to hurry away from their work to vote, often for a candidate whose name they hadn't heard before, and whom they selected at haphazard; female clerks and waitresses got up extra early to get their voting done before starting off to their places of business. Society women found their arrangements impeded and upset by the continual necessity for attending the polling stations, and week-end parties and summer holidays became gradually a masculine luxury. As for Cairo and the Riviera, they were possible only for genuine invalids or people of enormous wealth, for the accumulation of £10 fines during a prolonged absence was a contingency that even ordinarily wealthy folk could hardly afford to risk.

It was not wonderful that the female disfranchisement agitation became a formidable movement. The No-Votes-for-Women League numbered its feminine adherents by the million; its colours, citron and old Dutch-madder, were flaunted everywhere, and its battle hymn, 'We don't want to Vote,' became a popular refrain. As the Government showed no signs of being impressed by peaceful persuasion, more violent methods came into vogue. Meetings were disturbed, Ministers were mobbed, policemen were bitten, and ordinary prison fare rejected, and on the eve of the anniversary of Trafalgar women bound themselves in tiers up the entire length of the Nelson column so that its customary floral decoration had to be abandoned. Still the Government obstinately adhered to its conviction that women ought to have the vote.

Then, as a last resort, some woman wit hit upon an expedient which it was strange that no one had thought of before. The Great Weep was organized. Relays of women, ten thousand at a time, wept continuously in the public places of the Metropolis. They wept in railway stations, in tubes and omnibuses, in the National Gallery, at the Army and Navy Stores, in St. James's Park, at ballad concerts, at Prince's and in the Burlington Arcade. The hitherto unbroken success of the brilliant farcical comedy 'Henry's Rabbit' was imperilled by the presence of drearily weeping women in stalls and circle and gallery, and one of the brightest divorce cases that had been tried for many years was robbed of much of its sparkle by the lachrymose behaviour of a section of the audience.

'What are we to do?' asked the Prime Minister, whose cook had wept into all the breakfast dishes and whose nursemaid had gone out, crying quietly and miserably, to take the children for a walk in the Park.

'There is a time for everything,' said the King; 'there is a time to yield. Pass a measure through the two Houses depriving women of the right to vote, and bring it to me for the Royal assent the day after to-morrow.'

As the Minister withdrew, Hermann the Irascible, who was also nicknamed the Wise, gave a profound chuckle.

'There are more ways of killing a cat than by choking it with cream,' he quoted, 'but I'm not sure,' he added, 'that it's not the best way.'

19

THE QUEST

An unwonted peace hung over the Villa Elsinore, broken, however, at frequent intervals, by clamorous lamentations suggestive of bewildered bereavement. The Momebys had lost their infant child; hence the peace which its absence entailed; they were looking for it in wild, undisciplined fashion, giving tongue the whole time, which accounted for the outcry which swept through house and garden whenever they returned to try the home coverts anew. Clovis, who was temporarily and unwillingly a paying guest at the villa, had been dozing in a hammock at the far end of the garden when Mrs Momeby had broken the news to him.

'We've lost Baby,' she screamed.

'Do you mean that it's dead, or stampeded, or that you staked it at cards and lost it that way?' asked Clovis lazily.

'He was toddling about quite happily on the lawn,' said Mrs Momeby tearfully, 'and Arnold had just come in, and I was asking him what sort of sauce he would like with the asparagus—'

'I hope he said hollandaise,' interrupted Clovis, with a show of quickened interest, 'because if there's anything I hate—'

'And all of a sudden I missed Baby,' continued Mrs Momeby in a shriller tone. 'We've hunted high and low, in house and garden and outside the gates, and he's nowhere to be seen.'

'Is he anywhere to be heard?' asked Clovis; 'if not, he must be at least two miles away.'

'But where? And how?' asked the distracted mother.

'Perhaps an eagle or a wild beast has carried him off,' suggested Clovis.

'There aren't eagles and wild beasts in Surrey,' said Mrs Momeby, but a note of horror had crept into her voice.

'They escape now and then from travelling shows. Sometimes I think they let them get loose for the sake of the advertisement. Think what a sensational headline it would make in the local papers: 'Infant son of prominent Nonconformist devoured by spotted hyaena.' Your husband isn't a prominent Nonconformist, but his mother came of Wesleyan stock, and you must allow the newspapers some latitude.'

'But we should have found his remains,' sobbed Mrs Momeby.

'If the hyaena was really hungry and not merely toying with his food there wouldn't be much in the way of remains. It would be like the small-boy-and-apple story—there ain't going to be no core.'

Mrs Momeby turned away hastily to seek comfort and counsel in some other direction. With the selfish absorption of young motherhood she entirely disregarded Clovis's obvious anxiety about the asparagus sauce. Before she had gone a yard, however, the click of the side gate caused her to pull up sharp. Miss Gilpet, from the Villa Peterhof, had come over to hear details of the bereavement. Clovis was already rather bored with the story, but Mrs Momeby was equipped with that merciless faculty which finds as much joy in the ninetieth time of telling as in the first.

'Arnold had just come in; he was complaining of rheumatism—'

'There are so many things to complain of in this household that it would never have occurred to me to complain of rheumatism,' murmured Clovis.

'He was complaining of rheumatism,' continued Mrs Momeby, trying to throw a chilling inflection into a voice that was already doing a good deal of sobbing and talking at high pressure as well.

She was again interrupted.

'There is no such thing as rheumatism,' said Miss Gilpet. She said it with the conscious air of defiance that a waiter adopts in announcing that the cheapest-priced claret in the wine-list is no more. She did not proceed, however, to offer the alternative of some more expensive malady, but denied the existence of them all.

Mrs Momeby's temper began to shine out through her grief.

'I suppose you'll say next that Baby hasn't really disappeared.'

'He has disappeared,' conceded Miss Gilpet, 'but only because you haven't sufficient faith to find him. It's only lack of faith on your part that prevents him from being restored to you safe and well.'

'But if he's been eaten in the meantime by a hyaena and partly digested,' said Clovis, who clung affectionately to his wild beast theory, 'surely some ill-effects would be noticeable?'

Miss Gilpet was rather staggered by this complication of the question.

'I feel sure that a hyaena has not eaten him,' she said lamely.

'The hyaena may be equally certain that it has. You see, it may have just as much faith as you have, and more special knowledge as to the present whereabouts of the baby.'

Mrs Momeby was in tears again. 'If you have faith,' she sobbed, struck by a happy inspiration, 'won't you find our little Erik for us? I am sure you have powers that are denied to us.'

Rose-Marie Gilpet was thoroughly sincere in her adherence to Christian Science principles; whether she understood or correctly expounded them the learned in such matters may best decide. In the present case she was undoubtedly confronted with a great opportunity, and as she started forth on her vague search she strenuously summoned to her aid every scrap of faith that she possessed. She passed out into the bare and open high road, followed by Mrs Momeby's warning, 'It's no use going there, we've searched there a dozen times.' But Rose-Marie's ears were already deaf to all things save self-congratulation; for sitting in the middle of the highway, playing contentedly with the dust and some faded buttercups, was a white-pinafored baby with a mop of tow-coloured hair tied over one temple with a pale-blue ribbon. Taking first the usual feminine precaution of looking to see that no motor-car was on the distant horizon, Rose-Marie dashed at the child and bore it, despite its vigorous opposition, in through the portals of Elsinore. The child's furious screams had already announced the fact of its discovery, and the almost hysterical parents raced down the lawn to meet their restored offspring. The aesthetic value of the scene was marred in some degree by Rose-Marie's difficulty in holding the struggling infant, which was borne wrong-end foremost towards the agitated bosom of its family. 'Our own little Erik come back to us,' cried the Momebys in unison; as the child had rammed its fists tightly into its eye-sockets and nothing could be seen of its face but a widely gaping mouth, the recognition was in itself almost an act of faith.

'Is he glad to get back to Daddy and Mummy again?' crooned Mrs Momeby; the preference which the child was showing for its dust and buttercup distractions was so marked that the question struck Clovis as being unnecessarily tactless.

'Give him a ride on the roly-poly,' suggested the father brilliantly, as the howls continued with no sign of early abatement. In a moment the child had been placed astride the big garden roller and a preliminary tug was given to set it in motion. From the hollow depths of the cylinder came an earsplitting roar, drowning even the vocal efforts of the squalling baby, and immediately afterwards there crept forth a white-pinafored infant with a mop of tow-coloured hair tied over one temple with a pale blue ribbon. There was no mistaking either the features or the lung-power of the new arrival.

'Our own little Erik,' screamed Mrs Momeby, pouncing on

him and nearly smothering him with kisses; 'did he hide in the roly-poly to give us all a big fright?'

This was the obvious explanation of the child's sudden disappearance and equally abrupt discovery. There remained, however, the problem of the interloping baby, which now sat whimpering on the lawn in a disfavour as chilling as its previous popularity had been unwelcome. The Momebys glared at it as though it had wormed its way into their short-lived affections by heartless and unworthy pretences. Miss Gilpet's face took on an ashen tinge as she stared helplessly at the bunched-up figure that had been such a gladsome sight to her eyes a few moments ago.

'When love is over, how little of love even the lover understands,' quoted Clovis to himself.

Rose-Marie was the first to break the silence.

'If that is Erik you have in your arms, who is—that?'

'That, I think, is for you to explain,' said Mrs Momeby stiffly.

'Obviously,' said Clovis, 'it's a duplicate Erik that your powers of faith called into being. The question is: What are you going to do with him?'

The ashen pallor deepened in Rose-Marie's cheeks. Mrs Momeby clutched the genuine Erik closer to her side, as though she feared that her uncanny neighbour might out of sheer pique turn him into a bowl of gold-fish.

'I found him sitting in the middle of the road,' said Rose-Marie weakly.

'You can't take him back and leave him there,' said Clovis; 'the highway is meant for traffic, not to be used as a lumber-room for disused miracles.'

Rose-Marie wept. The proverb 'Weep and you weep alone,' broke down as badly on application as most of its kind. Both babies were wailing lugubriously, and the parent Momebys had scarcely recovered from their earlier lachrymose condition. Clovis alone maintained an unruffled cheerfulness.

'Must I keep him always?' asked Rose-Marie dolefully.

'Not always,' said Clovis consolingly; 'he can go into the Navy when he's thirteen.' Rose-Marie wept afresh.

'Of course,' added Clovis, 'there may be no end of a bother about his birth certificate. You'll have to explain matters to the Admiralty, and they're dreadfully hidebound.'

It was rather a relief when a breathless nursemaid from the Villa Charlottenburg over the way came running across the lawn to claim little Percy, who had slipped out of the front gate and disappeared like a twinkling from the high road.

And even then Clovis found it necessary to go in person to the kitchen to make sure about the asparagus sauce.

20

FILBOID STUDGE, THE STORY OF A MOUSE THAT HELPED

'I want to marry your daughter,' said Mark Spayley with faltering eagerness. 'I am only an artist with an income of two hundred a year, and she is the daughter of an enormously wealthy man, so I suppose you will think my offer a piece of presumption.'

Duncan Dullamy, the great company inflator, showed no outward sign of displeasure. As a matter of fact, he was secretly relieved at the prospect of finding even a two-hundred-a-year husband for his daughter Leonore. A crisis was rapidly rushing upon him, from which he knew he would emerge with neither money nor credit; all his recent ventures had fallen flat, and flattest of all had gone the wonderful new breakfast food, Pipenta, on the advertisement of which he had sunk such huge sums. It could scarcely be called a drug in the market; people bought drugs, but no one bought Pipenta.

'Would you marry Leonore if she were a poor man's daughter?' asked the man of phantom wealth.

'Yes,' said Mark, wisely avoiding the error of over-protestation. And to his astonishment Leonore's father not only gave his consent, but suggested a fairly early date for the wedding.

'I wish I could show my gratitude in some way,' said Mark with genuine emotion. 'I'm afraid it's rather like the mouse proposing to help the lion.'

'Get people to buy that beastly muck,' said Dullamy, nodding savagely at a poster of the despised Pipenta, 'and you'll have done more than any of my agents have been able to accomplish.'

'It wants a better name,' said Mark reflectively, 'and something distinctive in the poster line. Anyway, I'll have a shot at it.'

Three weeks later the world was advised of the coming of a new breakfast food, heralded under the resounding name of 'Filboid Studge.' Spayley put forth no pictures of massive babies springing up with fungus-like rapidity under its forcing influence, or of representatives of the leading nations of the world scrambling with fatuous eagerness for its possession. One huge sombre poster depicted the Damned in Hell suffering a new torment from their inability to get at the Filboid Studge which elegant young fiends held in transparent bowls just beyond their reach. The scene was rendered even more gruesome by a subtle suggestion of the features of leading men and women of the day in the portrayal of the Lost Souls; prominent individuals of both political parties, Society hostesses, well-known dramatic authors and novelists, and distinguished aeroplanists were dimly recognizable in that doomed throng; noted lights of the musical-comedy stage flickered wanly in the shades of the Inferno, smiling still from force of habit, but with the fearsome smiling rage of baffled effort. The poster bore no fulsome allusions to the merits of the new breakfast food, but a single grim statement ran in bold letters along its base: 'They cannot buy it now.'

Spayley had grasped the fact that people will do things from a sense of duty which they would never attempt as a pleasure. There are thousands of respectable middle-class men who, if you found them unexpectedly in a Turkish bath, would explain in all sincerity that a doctor had ordered them to take Turkish baths; if you told them in return that you went there because you liked it, they would stare in pained wonder at the frivolity of your motive. In the same way, whenever a massacre of Armenians is reported from Asia Minor, every one assumes that it has been carried out 'under orders' from somewhere or another, no one seems to think that there are people who might LIKE to kill their neighbours now and then.

And so it was with the new breakfast food. No one would have eaten Filboid Studge as a pleasure, but the grim austerity of its advertisement drove housewives in shoals to the grocers' shops to clamour for an immediate supply. In small kitchens solemn pig-tailed daughters helped depressed mothers to perform the primitive ritual of its preparation. On the breakfast-tables of cheerless parlours it was partaken of in silence. Once the womenfolk discovered that it was thoroughly unpalatable, their zeal in forcing it on their households knew no bounds. 'You haven't eaten your Filboid Studge!' would be screamed at the appetiteless clerk as he hurried weariedly from the breakfast-table, and his evening meal would be prefaced by a warmed-up mess which would be explained as 'your Filboid Studge that you didn't eat this morning.' Those strange fanatics who ostentatiously mortify themselves, inwardly and outwardly, with health biscuits and health garments, battened aggressively on the new food. Earnest, spectacled young men devoured it on the steps of the National Liberal Club. A bishop who did not believe in a future state preached against the poster, and a peer's daughter died from eating too much of the compound. A further advertisement was obtained when an infantry regiment mutinied and shot its officers rather than eat the nauseous mess; fortunately, Lord Birrell of Blatherstone, who was War Minister at the moment, saved the situation by his happy epigram, that 'Discipline to be effective must be optional.'

Filboid Studge had become a household word, but Dullamy wisely realized that it was not necessarily the last word in breakfast dietary; its supremacy would be challenged as soon as some yet more unpalatable food should be put on the market. There might even be a reaction in favour of something tasty and appetizing, and the Puritan austerity of the moment might be banished from domestic cookery. At an opportune moment, therefore, he sold out his interests in the article which had brought him in colossal wealth at a critical juncture, and placed his financial reputation beyond the reach of cavil. As for Leonore, who was now an heiress on a far greater scale than ever before, he naturally found her something a vast deal higher in the husband market than a two-hundred-a-year poster designer. Mark Spayley, the brainmouse who had helped the financial lion with such untoward effect, was left to curse the day he produced the wonder-working poster.

'After all,' said Clovis, meeting him shortly afterwards at his club, 'you have this doubtful consolation, that 'tis not in mortals to countermand success.'

21

THE OPEN WINDOW

'My aunt will be down presently, Mr Nuttel,' said a very self-possessed young lady of fifteen; 'in the meantime you must try and put up with me.'

Framton Nuttel endeavoured to say the correct something which should duly flatter the niece of the moment without unduly discounting the aunt that was to come. Privately he doubted more than ever whether these formal visits on a succession of total strangers would do much towards helping the nerve cure which he was supposed to be undergoing.

'I know how it will be,' his sister had said when he was preparing to migrate to this rural retreat; 'you will bury yourself down there and not speak to a living soul, and your nerves will be worse than ever from moping. I shall just give you letters of introduction to all the people I know there. Some of them, as far as I can remember, were quite nice.'

Framton wondered whether Mrs Sappleton, the lady to whom he was presenting one of the letters of introduction came into the nice division.

'Do you know many of the people round here?' asked the niece, when she judged that they had had sufficient silent communion.

'Hardly a soul,' said Framton. 'My sister was staying here,

at the rectory, you know, some four years ago, and she gave me letters of introduction to some of the people here.'

He made the last statement in a tone of distinct regret.

'Then you know practically nothing about my aunt?' pursued the self-possessed young lady.

'Only her name and address,' admitted the caller. He was wondering whether Mrs Sappleton was in the married or widowed state. An undefinable something about the room seemed to suggest masculine habitation.

'Her great tragedy happened just three years ago,' said the child; 'that would be since your sister's time.'

'Her tragedy?' asked Framton; somehow in this restful country spot tragedies seemed out of place.

'You may wonder why we keep that window wide open on an October afternoon,' said the niece, indicating a large French window that opened on to a lawn.

'It is quite warm for the time of the year,' said Framton; 'but has that window got anything to do with the tragedy?'

'Out through that window, three years ago to a day, her husband and her two young brothers went off for their day's shooting. They never came back. In crossing the moor to their favourite snipe-shooting ground they were all three engulfed in a treacherous piece of bog. It had been that dreadful wet summer, you know, and places that were safe in other years gave way suddenly without warning. Their bodies were never recovered. That was the dreadful part of it.' Here the child's voice lost its self-possessed note and became falteringly human. 'Poor aunt always thinks that they will come back someday, they and the little brown spaniel that was lost with them, and walk in at that window just as they used to do. That is why the window is kept open every evening till it is quite dusk. Poor dear aunt, she has often told me how they went out, her husband with his white waterproof coat over his arm, and Ronnie, her youngest brother, singing 'Bertie, why do you bound?' as he always did to tease her, because she said it got on her nerves. Do you know, sometimes on still, quiet evenings like this, I almost get a creepy feeling that they will all walk in through that window—'

She broke off with a little shudder. It was a relief to Framton when the aunt bustled into the room with a whirl of apologies for being late in making her appearance.

'I hope Vera has been amusing you?' she said.

'She has been very interesting,' said Framton.

'I hope you don't mind the open window,' said Mrs Sappleton briskly; 'my husband and brothers will be home directly from shooting, and they always come in this way. They've been out for snipe in the marshes today, so they'll make a fine mess over my poor carpets. So like you menfolk, isn't it?'

She rattled on cheerfully about the shooting and the scarcity of birds, and the prospects for duck in the winter. To Framton it was all purely horrible. He made a desperate but only partially successful effort to turn the talk on to a less ghastly topic, he was conscious that his hostess was giving him only a fragment of her attention, and her eyes were constantly straying past him to the open window and the lawn beyond. It was certainly an unfortunate coincidence that he should have paid his visit on this tragic anniversary.

'The doctors agree in ordering me complete rest, an absence of mental excitement, and avoidance of anything in the nature of violent physical exercise,' announced Framton, who laboured under the tolerably widespread delusion that total strangers and chance acquaintances are hungry for the least detail of one's ailments and infirmities, their cause and cure. 'On the matter of diet they are not so much in agreement,' he continued.

'No?' said Mrs Sappleton, in a voice which only replaced a yawn at the last moment. Then she suddenly brightened into alert attention—but not to what Framton was saying.

'Here they are at last!' she cried. 'Just in time for tea, and don't they look as if they were muddy up to the eyes!'

Framton shivered slightly and turned towards the niece with a look intended to convey sympathetic comprehension. The child was staring out through the open window with a dazed horror in her eyes. In a chill shock of nameless fear Framton swung round in his seat and looked in the same direction.

In the deepening twilight three figures were walking across the lawn towards the window, they all carried guns under their arms, and one of them was additionally burdened with a white coat hung over his shoulders. A tired brown spaniel kept close at their heels. Noiselessly they neared the house, and then a hoarse young voice chanted out of the dusk: 'I said, Bertie, why do you bound?'

Framton grabbed wildly at his stick and hat; the hall door, the gravel drive, and the front gate were dimly noted stages in his headlong retreat. A cyclist coming along the road had to run into the hedge to avoid imminent collision.

'Here we are, my dear,' said the bearer of the white mackintosh, coming in through the window, 'fairly muddy, but most of it's dry. Who was that who bolted out as we came up?'

'A most extraordinary man, a Mr Nuttel,' said Mrs Sappleton; 'could only talk about his illnesses, and dashed off without a word of goodby or apology when you arrived. One would think he had seen a ghost.'

'I expect it was the spaniel,' said the niece calmly; 'he told me he had a horror of dogs. He was once hunted into a cemetery somewhere on the banks of the Ganges by a pack of pariah dogs, and had to spend the night in a newly dug grave with the creatures snarling and grinning and foaming just above him. Enough to make anyone lose their nerve.'

Romance at short notice was her speciality.

22

THE UNREST-CURE

On the rack in the railway carriage immediately opposite Clovis was a solidly wrought travelling bag, with a carefully written label, on which was inscribed, 'J. P. Huddle, The Warren, Tilfield, near Slowborough.' Immediately below the rack sat the human embodiment of the label, a solid, sedate individual, sedately dressed, sedately conversational. Even without his conversation (which was addressed to a friend seated by his side, and touched chiefly on such topics as the backwardness of Roman hyacinths and the prevalence of measles at the Rectory), one could have gauged fairly accurately the temperament and mental outlook of the travelling bag's owner. But he seemed unwilling to leave anything to the imagination of a casual observer, and his talk grew presently personal and introspective.

'I don't know how it is,' he told his friend, 'I'm not much over forty, but I seem to have settled down into a deep groove of elderly middle-age. My sister shows the same tendency. We like everything to be exactly in its accustomed place; we like things to happen exactly at their appointed times; we like everything to be usual, orderly, punctual, methodical, to a hair's breadth, to a minute. It distresses and upsets us if it is not so. For instance, to take a very trifling matter, a thrush has built its nest year after year in the catkin-tree on the lawn; this year, for no obvious reason, it is building in the ivy on the garden wall. We have said very little about it, but I think we both feel that the change is unnecessary, and just a little irritating.'

'Perhaps,' said the friend, 'it is a different thrush.'

'We have suspected that,' said J. P. Huddle, 'and I think it gives us even more cause for annoyance. We don't feel that we want a change of thrush at our time of life; and yet, as I have said, we have scarcely reached an age when these things should make themselves seriously felt.'

'What you want,' said the friend, 'is an Unrest-cure.'

'An Unrest-cure? I've never heard of such a thing.'

'You've heard of Rest-cures for people who've broken down under stress of too much worry and strenuous living; well, you're suffering from overmuch repose and placidity, and you need the opposite kind of treatment.'

'But where would one go for such a thing?'

'Well, you might stand as an Orange candidate for Kilkenny, or do a course of district visiting in one of the Apache quarters of Paris, or give lectures in Berlin to prove that most of Wagner's music was written by Gambetta; and there's always the interior of Morocco to travel in. But, to be really effective, the Unrest-cure ought to be tried in the home. How you would do it I haven't the faintest idea.'

It was at this point in the conversation that Clovis became galvanized into alert attention. After all, his two days' visit to an elderly relative at Slowborough did not promise much excitement. Before the train had stopped he had decorated his sinister shirt-cuff with the inscription, 'J. P. Huddle, The Warren, Tilfield, near Slowborough.'

Two mornings later Mr Huddle broke in on his sister's privacy as she sat reading Country Life in the morning room. It was her day and hour and place for reading Country Life, and the intrusion was absolutely irregular; but he bore in his hand a telegram, and in that household telegrams were recognized as happening by the hand of God. This particular telegram partook of the nature of a thunderbolt. 'Bishop examining confirmation class in neighbourhood unable stay rectory on account measles invokes your hospitality sending secretary arrange.'

'I scarcely know the Bishop; I've only spoken to him once,' exclaimed J. P. Huddle, with the exculpating air of one who realizes too late the indiscretion of speaking to strange Bishops. Miss Huddle was the first to rally; she disliked thunderbolts as fervently as her brother did, but the womanly instinct in her told her that thunderbolts must be fed.

'We can curry the cold duck,' she said. It was not the appointed day for curry, but the little orange envelope involved a certain departure from rule and custom. Her brother said nothing, but his eyes thanked her for being brave.

'A young gentleman to see you,' announced the parlour-maid.

'The secretary!' murmured the Huddles in unison; they instantly stiffened into a demeanour which proclaimed that, though they held all strangers to be guilty, they were willing to hear anything they might have to say in their defence. The young gentleman, who came into the room with a certain elegant haughtiness, was not at all Huddle's idea of a bishop's secretary; he had not supposed that the episcopal establishment could have afforded such an expensively upholstered article when there were so many other claims on its resources. The face was fleetingly familiar; if he had bestowed more attention on the fellow-traveller sitting opposite him in the railway carriage two days before he might have recognized Clovis in his present visitor.

'You are the Bishop's secretary?' asked Huddle, becoming consciously deferential.

'His confidential secretary,' answered Clovis. 'You may call me Stanislaus; my other name doesn't matter. The Bishop and Colonel Alberti may be here to lunch. I shall be here in any case.'

It sounded rather like the programme of a Royal visit.

'The Bishop is examining a confirmation class in the neighbourhood, isn't he?' asked Miss Huddle.

'Ostensibly,' was the dark reply, followed by a request for a large-scale map of the locality.

Clovis was still immersed in a seemingly profound study of the map when another telegram arrived. It was addressed to 'Prince Stanislaus, care of Huddle, The Warren, etc.' Clovis glanced at the contents and announced: 'The Bishop and Alberti won't be here till late in the afternoon.' Then he returned to his scrutiny of the map.

The luncheon was not a very festive function. The princely secretary ate and drank with fair appetite, but severely discouraged conversation. At the finish of the meal he broke suddenly into a radiant smile, thanked his hostess for a charming repast, and kissed her hand with deferential rapture. Miss Huddle was unable to decide in her mind whether the action savoured of Louis Quatorzian courtliness or the reprehensible Roman attitude towards the Sabine women. It was not her day for having a headache, but she felt that the circumstances excused her, and retired to her room to have as much headache as was possible before the Bishop's arrival. Clovis, having asked the way to the nearest telegraph office, disappeared presently down the carriage drive. Mr Huddle met him in the hall some two hours later, and asked when the Bishop would arrive.

'He is in the library with Alberti,' was the reply.

'But why wasn't I told? I never knew he had come!' exclaimed Huddle.

'No one knows he is here,' said Clovis; 'the quieter we can keep matters the better. And on no account disturb him in the library. Those are his orders.'

'But what is all this mystery about? And who is Alberti? And isn't the Bishop going to have tea?'

'The Bishop is out for blood, not tea.'

'Blood!' gasped Huddle, who did not find that the thunderbolt improved on acquaintance.

'Tonight is going to be a great night in the history of Christendom,' said Clovis. 'We are going to massacre every Jew in the neighbourhood.'

'To massacre the Jews!' said Huddle indignantly. 'Do you mean to tell me there's a general rising against them?'

'No, it's the Bishop's own idea. He's in there arranging all the details now.'

'But—the Bishop is such a tolerant, humane man.'

'That is precisely what will heighten the effect of his action. The sensation will be enormous.'

That at least Huddle could believe.

'He will be hanged!' he exclaimed with conviction.

'A motor is waiting to carry him to the coast, where a steam yacht is in readiness.'

'But there aren't thirty Jews in the whole neighbourhood,' protested Huddle, whose brain, under the repeated shocks of the day, was operating with the uncertainty of a telegraph wire during earthquake disturbances.

'We have twenty-six on our list,' said Clovis, referring to a bundle of notes. 'We shall be able to deal with them all the more thoroughly.'

'Do you mean to tell me that you are meditating violence against a man like Sir Leon Birberry,' stammered Huddle; 'he's one of the most respected men in the country.'

'He's down on our list,' said Clovis carelessly; 'after all, we've got men we can trust to do our job, so we shan't have to rely on local assistance. And we've got some Boy-scouts helping us as auxiliaries.'

'Boy-scouts!'

'Yes; when they understood there was real killing to be done they were even keener than the men.'

'This thing will be a blot on the Twentieth Century!'

'And your house will be the blotting-pad. Have you realized that half the papers of Europe and the United States will publish pictures of it? By the way, I've sent some photographs of you and your sister, that I found in the library, to the Matin and Die Woche; I hope you don't mind. Also a sketch of the staircase; most of the killing will probably be done on the staircase.'

The emotions that were surging in J. P. Huddle's brain were almost too intense to be disclosed in speech, but he managed to gasp out: 'There aren't any Jews in this house.'

'Not at present,' said Clovis.

'I shall go to the police,' shouted Huddle with sudden energy.

'In the shrubbery,' said Clovis, 'are posted ten men, who have orders to fire on any one who leaves the house without my signal of permission. Another armed picquet is in ambush near the front gate. The Boy-scouts watch the back premises.'

At this moment the cheerful hoot of a motor-horn was heard from the drive. Huddle rushed to the hall door with the feeling of a man half-awakened from a nightmare, and beheld Sir Leon Birberry, who had driven himself over in his car. 'I got your telegram,' he said; 'what's up?'

Telegram? It seemed to be a day of telegrams.

'Come here at once. Urgent. James Huddle,' was the purport of the message displayed before Huddle's bewildered eyes.

'I see it all!' he exclaimed suddenly in a voice shaken with agitation, and with a look of agony in the direction of the shrubbery he hauled the astonished Birberry into the house. Tea had just been laid in the hall, but the now thoroughly panic-stricken Huddle dragged his protesting guest upstairs, and in a few minutes' time the entire household had been summoned to that region of momentary safety. Clovis alone graced the tea-table with his presence; the fanatics in the library were evidently too immersed in their monstrous machinations to dally with the solace of teacup and hot toast. Once the youth rose, in answer to the summons of the front-door bell, and admitted Mr Paul Isaacs, shoemaker and parish councillor, who had also received a pressing invitation to The Warren. With an atrocious assumption of courtesy, which a Borgia could hardly have outdone, the secretary escorted this new captive of his net to the head of the stairway, where his involuntary host awaited him.

And then ensued a long ghastly vigil of watching and waiting. Once or twice Clovis left the house to stroll across to the shrubbery, returning always to the library, for the purpose evidently of making a brief report. Once he took in the letters from the evening postman, and brought them to the top of the stairs with punctilious politeness. After his next absence he came half-way up the stairs to make an announcement.

'The Boy-scouts mistook my signal, and have killed the postman. I've had very little practice in this sort of thing, you see. Another time I shall do better.'

The housemaid, who was engaged to be married to the evening postman, gave way to clamorous grief.

'Remember that your mistress has a headache,' said J. P. Huddle. (Miss Huddle's headache was worse.)

Clovis hastened downstairs, and after a short visit to the library returned with another message:

'The Bishop is sorry to hear that Miss Huddle has a headache. He is issuing orders that as far as possible no firearms shall be used near the house; any killing that is necessary on the premises will be done with cold steel. The Bishop does not see why a man should not be a gentleman as well as a Christian.'

That was the last they saw of Clovis; it was nearly seven o'clock, and his elderly relative liked him to dress for dinner. But, though he had left them for ever, the lurking suggestion of his presence haunted the lower regions of the house during the long hours of the wakeful night, and every creak of the stairway, every rustle of wind through the shrubbery, was fraught with horrible meaning. At about seven next morning the gardener's boy and the early postman finally convinced the watchers that the Twentieth Century was still unblotted.

'I don't suppose,' mused Clovis, as an early train bore him townwards, 'that they will be in the least grateful for the Unrest-cure.'

ABOUT TERRY O'BRIEN

Terry O'Brien is an academic with three decades of experience in teaching language and communication skills in India and abroad. He also headed a college under the auspices of the University of Delhi.

A prolific writer, with several books to his credit, Terry O'Brien is a reputed professional motivational speaker and a quizmaster.

Printed in Germany
by Amazon Distribution
GmbH, Leipzig